WATCHING ANGELS

The Arts Council
An Chomhairle Ealaíon

First published in 2000 by
Marino Books
an imprint of Mercier Press
16 Hume Street Dublin 2
Tel: (01) 661 5299; Fax: (01) 661 8583
E.mail: books@marino.ie

Trade enquiries to CMD Distribution
55A Spruce Avenue
Stillorgan Industrial Park
Blackrock County Dublin
Tel: (01) 294 2556; Fax: (01) 294 2564
E.mail: cmd@columba.ie

© Kevin McDermott

ISBN 1 86023 110 1

10 9 8 7 6 5 4 3 2 1

A CIP record for this title is available
from the British Library

Cover design by SPACE
Printed in Ireland by ColourBooks
Baldoyle Dublin 13

June 2000
For Paddy.

WATCHING ANGELS

Kevin McDermott

KEVIN McDERMOTT

Acknowledgements

Two books were of particular help to me in writing the Renaissance sections of *Watching Angels*. Roger Jones and Nicholas Penny's *Raphael* (Yale, 1983) is an excellent introduction to the painter's work. The book contains Raphael's piortraits of many of the characters mentioned in *Watching Angels*, including the splendid portraits of Pope Julius II and Baldassare Castiglione. Castiglione's *The Book of the Courtier* (London, 1967) gives us an idealised portrait of the court of Urbino in 1507.

The Prague of Rudolph II is brilliantly evoked in Angelo Maria Ripellino's *Magic Prague*. I also dipped into Arthur Koestler's *The Sleepwalkers* (London 1959), with its eloquent accounts of both Kepler and Tycho Brahe.

I am sure that Primo Levi's *If This Is A Man* (London, 1965) influenced my account of Jacob and Maria's journey to Auschwitz. A conversation with Johnny Philips, who shared with me some of his family's history, gave me the idea for Jacob's visit to Prague and Dresden, fifty years after the war.

I want to thank Eileen Murphy, Patricia Branigan, John McDonnell and Deirdre Crofts for making my research in Rome and Florence so enjoyable; and Peter Caulwell and Adrienne Byrne in whose comany I visited Terezin.

Jo O'Donoghue and Sean O'Keeffe of Marino were helpful and encouraging.

My final word of thanks is to Mary Fagan who introduced me to Italy and to Prague.

for Aoife

Contents

Watching Angels

The painter created them,
Those watching angels.
And they looked out on the world,
Alarmed by what they saw.
And centuries came and went,
And endless seasons changed,
And trees leafed and unleafed,
And birds called and built their nests,
And light dawned and faded,
And still those watching angels
Saw all and did not forget.

1

A Request

Dublin, spring 1995

Jacob was sitting at a table in the café waiting for his son. He was early. He drank tea and thought about the scene to come.

There'd be tears. He'd play the tired old man. Dignified in his suffering. (He'd practised his expression in front of a mirror; there was no point in leaving anything to chance.) And his son would lay a comforting hand on his arm, embarrassed by his father's show of emotion. He'd play him for a time. Then make the announcement, 'I'm going away.' He foresaw his son's confused alarm.

He'd allow that to settle before explaining that he was going to Dresden. He'd wave away the protests.

'Why, after all these years?'

'There's nothing there for you.'

'You'll upset yourself.'

'You can't travel on your own.'

He'd feign hurt. Lower his eyes. Fidget with the spoon.

'Well perhaps Ben could come with me.'

He'd have to be careful. Make it seem like the suggestion came from the other side of the table. And his dutiful son would play the dutiful husband.

'I'll have to talk with Kim.'

His poor son. So safe, so predictable.

Jacob cut his scone and covered it in butter and jam. He lifted a piece to his mouth. A small blob of jam clung to the corner of his lip. The tip of his tongue found it and drew it inside.

'We'll go in early summer,' he said to himself, and smiled.

2

THE SEED OF AN IDEA

Montecastelo, 1510

The two figures moved slowly through the lines of vegetables. They pulled at the weeds that choked the young plants. They picked off the slugs that fed on the tender leaves. When the sun reached its height in the cloudless sky and the intense heat beat down upon them, the father straightened his back, wiped the sweat from his brow and signalled to his son to cease his labours. The boy stood upright. He stretched his arms above his head and shook the tiredness from his limbs. The two turned towards home.

'May I call in to Menocchio for a little time, father?' Andrea asked.

Enrico nodded his assent. He added, as the boy hurried away, 'Don't stay all day. There is more to be done. And don't listen to everything that madman tells you.'

But the boy was already out of hearing and his father contented himself with some dark mutterings.

*

It was Menocchio who had first spoken of angels to Andrea.

'Consider, young master,' he began one day, no sooner than the boy had entered the storeroom, 'Gabriel, the chief messenger of God. How did he come to the Virgin? Did he fly down from heaven, through all the vastness and darkness of the skies, propelling himself forward with his wings? Or was he hovering close to Mary's dwelling all the time, invisible to her eye, awaiting God's instruction? And if he was, did he materialise before her like a figure in a dream? What do you think, Andrea?'

Here the miller paused, lost in thought. Then he resumed, 'Or did he come into her presence in a great rush of air, frightening the Virgin before she understood who it was had come before her? Well, young master, what answers have you for me? Tell me!'

And Andrea, taken aback by the compelling tone of the miller's question, spluttered, 'I don't know, Menocchio.'

'Ah, you young people, is there nothing in your heads? Does the curate teach you anything in those classes of his?'

'Not much about angels, I'm afraid,' Andrea replied timidly.

And the miller smiled. 'Well take a seat, young master, and I will teach you about angels.'

And thus began Andrea's education at the hands of Menocchio the miller.

Andrea called into the mill most days. Today Menocchio was weighing out sacks of grain in the storeroom. He was whistling, and he saluted Andrea heartily as the boy entered.

'Ah, my young genius is come to keep me company,' he observed good-humouredly. 'Here, twist the stays around the neck of the filled sacks. Make yourself useful, young master.' Menocchio gestured towards the leather strips which lay on a deep window ledge. Andrea took one and began securing the prepared sacks of flour. The room where they worked was whitewashed, and the sun streamed through the narrow windows in great dazzling shafts of light in which dust particles floated and shimmered.

Andrea loved the busy atmosphere of the mill. He loved the slow movement of the stone grinder, the rumble of the machinery, the movement of the cogwheels and the muted sound of the waterwheel, which set everything in motion. Andrea loved Menocchio's good humour, his insatiable appetite for talk and argument, his inventive imagination and his stories. Sometimes the boy came and sat drawing in the storeroom, using bits of chalk or lumps of charcoal – or any material he could lay his hands on. Menocchio encouraged Andrea and defended him against the charge of laziness, which the boy's father sometimes laid against his son, for Andrea's father worked ceaselessly to make his small farm support his family.

The farm was owned by the local lord, Signor Datini. Andrea's father, Enrico, supplied the labour and the profit was divided between landlord and farmer. Enrico kept a cow and some chickens, but the main produce of the farm was wheat, with some olives and grapes. A vegetable garden ensured an ample supply of fresh produce for both lord and tenant.

'Some day, Enrico,' the miller declared, 'this boy of yours will be a famous painter, mark my words, and Menocchio will boast that he alone recognised his early genius.'

'In the meantime, Menocchio, the chickens need

feeding and the fields need planting!'

'There is more to life, Enrico, than chickens and vegetables! Let the boy be!'

Menocchio was all movement and energy. He was small and light-framed for a miller, but his body was strong and muscular and he pulled, lifted and dragged sacks of grain as effortlessly as a man twice his size would have done. He was full of mischief, teasing the women who came to buy his flour and complaining to the farmers who supplied the grain. Menocchio had no family of his own, so he felt free to comment on everyone else's.

Not all the villagers and peasants from the surrounding countryside liked Menocchio. True, he was a first-class miller, but many considered him too big for his boots – a man of no education who held an opinion on every subject under the sun. Moreover, Menocchio spoke without discretion when farmers came at harvest time with their grain. The miller liked nothing better than to raise a laugh and did so by expressing outrageous ideas. He mocked the Church's teachings on heaven and hell. He denied the existence of the soul. He declared that the Pope and the bishops were not the guardians of Christ's teaching. Farmers laughed but Menocchio, with his loose talk, gave his enemies a stick with which to beat him. And though he was scrupulously honest in measuring flour and paying a just amount to the peasants for their grain, he suffered from the general suspicion felt against millers, who were commonly regarded as the greatest thieves in Christendom. So it was no great surprise when a representative from the bishop called on Menocchio to quiz him on his religious beliefs and to remind him of the punishment that was meted out to convicted heretics.

This visit alarmed Menocchio, and he attended to his religious duties with great care for many months afterwards, being sure to be seen at Mass and making a point of going to Confession and receiving Communion. But behind this show of devotion and obedience he was as rebellious and disbelieving as ever. He shared his innermost thoughts with Andrea, who, young as he was, kept the miller's confidence.

Menocchio speculated endlessly on the identity of the person who had reported him to the bishop. There were many possible suspects, and the miller began to bear a grudge against them all. And his bitterness grew and grew.

So when Andrea entered the mill on that bright summer's day, he was not surprised when the miller's talk turned to a theme he had rehearsed more and more frequently.

'Do not stay in this place, Andrea. It is a nest of vipers. Go out into the world, for there is a great world beyond these hills, a world where men's minds are large and filled with stories and imaginings. And there are worlds beyond the seas, with more marvels than you or I ever dreamed of. There are the eastern lands visited by the great Marco Polo. Go east and prosper, Andrea. Leave this place!'

'But how, Menocchio? What can I do? Where can I go?'

And there was such pleading in the boy's answer that Menocchio stopped his work and looked steadily at his young companion. The miller spoke quietly.

'It is possible for you to leave here, Andrea. To begin with, you will go to . . . ' The miller frowned, searching his mind. 'Yes!' he declared triumphantly, stabbing the air with his finger. 'You will go to Urbino, to the school there.' The miller paused to consider his own suggestion. 'It is said that the school is open to all boys, regardless of wealth or distinction. Poor scholars and young noblemen study side by side. They read the great authors, are taught mathematics and learn how to become courtiers. In Urbino you will learn all that you need to know to make your way in the world. And you will meet the fine gentlemen of the world there. Then you can go and serve in the courts of the mighty and paint for them or travel the oceans at their bidding.'

Menocchio paused, dazzled by the future he saw unfolding for his young friend. Andrea dared not let himself believe that such things were possible. He refused to be seduced by the miller's talk. There was a challenge in his voice when he spoke.

'And why, Menocchio, would they admit me, Andrea Doni, to this academy? Who am I? I am nothing. Don't talk of what can never be.'

The miller was stung by Andrea's words, and he spoke with a trembling voice.

'Do you think I trifle with you, young master? Do you think I make fun of you? No. I tell you, you can find a place in the school in Urbino. Who else can draw as you can? There is no one in this village or in any of the surrounding villages who can match you. And you are strong and handsome, Andrea. You know how to speak well and, more importantly, you know when to keep your mouth shut. True, I am only a miller but I am not a stupid man and I can distinguish the chaff from the wheat. You will find a place in Urbino because you deserve the chance.'

The miller's words tumbled out in a rush of justification and energy. When he had finished he sat down on a little stool across from Andrea. The boy dropped his head in embarrassment at the miller's vehemence. The miller continued in a measured tone and with authority, though in reality he knew little of life in Urbino.

'In the ducal palace are gathered the greatest painters and architects, for the court is the finest in the land. And the duke is related to the Pope himself. You will find no better place to begin your education.' The miller nodded his head. 'Yes, we must arrange for the duke or his representative to meet you.'

'But who will speak for me, Menocchio? My father is a good man, but . . . It is impossible, Menocchio. Should my father take his donkey and travel to Urbino and knock on the palace door and ask to see the duke? What you have said about Urbino is fine, beautiful talk, Menocchio, but it is only talk.'

The miller did not reply for a little time, and when he did there was steel in his tone. 'You are wrong, Andrea. The lord of our village will speak for you. I will ask him to sponsor you. If he writes to the duke, the duke will take note. I am not without influence in this village. Within the year, we will have you in Urbino!'

Andrea smiled, believing and not believing what the miller said.

But Menocchio was true to his word, and determined. He spoke to the lord of the village and the lord wrote to the duke:

Permit me, Your Excellency, to introduce to you Andrea Doni, son of Enrico Doni of Montecastelo. The boy has been known to me since his birth. The curate and the men of learning in this area consider him a scholar and well gifted in the art of drawing.

Andrea Doni is a good youth and comes from a respectable family. He is polite, sensible and well spoken. He brings honour to his family and his village.

The boy has learned all that we can teach him in Montecastelo, but he is such a promising youth that I beg you to admit him to your academy in Urbino. One day he will bring great praise and honour upon you.

In all regards I am your humble servant.
Giovanni Datini

This letter was sealed and in time found its way into the hands of the Duke of Urbino, Francesco Maria della Rovere, nephew of the Pope and ruler of a city renowned in all Christendom for its learning and sophistication. Francesco was no equal to his immediate predecessors as either a scholar or a statesman, though.

The duke took note of the letter from Montecastelo. Why? Because, it is said, the boy's name was Andrea, the same as the duke's son who had died in infancy. And it is said that, in a rush of drunken sentiment, Francesco dictated a letter saying that a place would be found for Andrea in the court of Urbino if he satisfied the chief courtiers of his potential. The letter was sent and the affair was promptly forgotten by the duke.

The reply from the duke neglected to tell Signor Datini that the Academy of Urbino had lapsed with the death of Francesco's grand-uncle Federico Da Montefeltro. Nor did the letter give any hint that the duke was a man of uneven and sometimes violent temper. But Menocchio had achieved his aim, for the Duke of Urbino replied to the letter and invited Andrea to come to the palace, where a place would be found for him. And Andrea, who was quick, observant and careful, would learn all that Menocchio wished him to learn.

Thus it came to pass that, three months after Menocchio had first mentioned it, days after the boy's fourteenth birthday, Andrea arrived with his father at the palace at Urbino in the little farm cart pulled by the family's old donkey.

3

A RAID

Outside Berlin, February 1944

The early-morning sun shone on the woodland. From the air all might have been observed. The outer walls of the demesne. Oak and beech trees planted in a circle around the house. The sunlight breaking through the canopy of leaves. Among the trees, dark forms moving across the face of the earth. And the silence, broken by the occasional birdcall.

The procession continued quietly, stealthily. The grey and black figures were sure-footed. As they neared the edge of the woods, the advance came to a halt. The commandant checked the lines and then signalled to his lieutenants to begin the final approach.

One by one, soldiers broke from cover and raced up to the house. Each one positioned himself next to a window. They stood like toy soldiers, their backs to the wall, rifles across their chests, ready to swing round and discharge their weapons at the enemy within. As soon as the cordon was complete, the commandant, flanked by two escorts, marched briskly up the steps to the double doors and beat upon them with the butt of his revolver. The sound died, the wood absorbing the blows and throwing out no echo. The silence held.

There was no commotion from within, no scurrying steps, no shouts or screams of panic. The commandant knocked again. He leant against the door, trying the handle. Nothing happened. At his word, one of the escorts shot away the lock with a burst of gunfire. The door swung open.

There was a moment's hesitation. The smoke from the shooting dissipated. The silence composed itself again. Cautiously, the commandant entered the house. He gripped his gun tightly. The floorboards creaked under the pressure of his boots. Aiming the pistol, the officer surveyed the upper storey, expecting a salvo of bullets to be directed at him at any moment. But it did not come. He stood still, listening, his gaze directed upwards to the high ceiling and its elaborate plasterwork. Perplexed, he went back to the entrance and summoned a lieutenant to advance with his men. The soldiers were sent searching through the house. Within a minute there was a flurry of activity and the commandant was called to inspect what had been discovered in the library on the first floor.

He reached the room at a trot. Inside, the shutters were closed against the light and he could see little. As he advanced into the room, he caught a distinct smell of leather and wax. And then he drew up sharply. In the centre of the room a group of people, ten or more, sat quietly at a circular table. Their silent presence startled him.

'Get up, get up,' he commanded, brusquely. There was no response.

'They are dead, Herr Commandant,' a soldier whispered nervously.

'Dead?'

The soldier nodded.

The commandant walked forward to the table and touched a woman on the shoulder. She slumped sideways in her chair. He felt cold and shivered involuntarily. He was amused at his own reaction. He, who had lived with violent death for many years, was frightened by the calm air of the dead sitting so comfortably at their table. He thought the situation hysterically funny, though he betrayed none of his feelings to his men. He ordered the shutters to be opened and the light fell on the old people, four women and six men.

A bearded man wore his Jewish skullcap and a shawl fringed at the corners. Before him a book lay open. The commandant looked over his shoulder at the text. It was a psalm. His eyes roamed over the words: 'The Lord is my shepherd; there is nothing I shall want. He maketh me lie down in green pastures; he leadeth me beside the still waters.'

He stood, pensive, for a moment in the quiet stillness, but the hush which had settled in the room was broken by the sound of gunfire and shouting from outside the house. The commandant surveyed the scene from the window. Soldiers were running and a man lay face-down on the grass just in front of the woods.

The noise and commotion banished the solemnity from the room. 'Burn all this,' he ordered his lieutenant – indicating, with the slightest movement of his head, the group at the table – as he hurried outside into the fresh air.

A young officer stood over the body of the prone man. The commandant was stern.

'What happened?' he asked.

'This man made a run from the house. He was ordered to stop and, when he failed to do so, I shot him,' the young man explained. There was no hiding the anxiety in his voice.

The commandant touched the body with his foot. 'Turn him over.'

The officer bent down and, gripping the dead man by the shoulder, turned him onto his back.

'Is it the suspect?' the younger man enquired of his superior.

'Yes, this is Benjamin Philip. He would have been useful to us.'

'There was little time to think, Herr Commandant.'

The commandant turned away, without a word. And then, as if reconsidering the matter, he turned back and aimed a single kick at the body lying before him.

'None of us can rest easy until the threat of the Jew is removed. Remember that. They have stolen what rightly belongs to every German citizen. Take some men and burn him along with the others.'

'The others, Herr Commandant?'

'Yes, there are others in the house.'

He surveyed the sky. 'Philip, I suspect, put the old ones to sleep. I doubt they knew what he was doing. They would not have given their consent. Their God, you see, does not allow them such mercies. Only he has the power to give and take life.' The commandant smiled. 'We have taken upon ourselves the role of God.'

He looked at his officer. His tone was ironic, mocking.

'Does the life you have taken make you a god of the Jews?'

The young man smiled uncertainly.

'Well?' his superior persisted.

The lieutenant shifted nervously under the commandant's scrutiny.

'I don't believe so, sir,' he ventured at last.

'Good. It is not wise to believe that you are immortal. It tempts fate.' The commanding officer's features went through the motions of breaking into a smile. 'Have the car brought round.'

'Yes, Herr Commandant.'

The commandant walked away from the scene to a spot where the sun shone brightly on the grass. He took a packet of cigarettes from his breast pocket and deftly removed one. He lit it and smoked thoughtfully. Above him there was lark song. As he was driven down the avenue, he looked back and saw wreaths of smoke rise above the trees. He closed his eyes and dozed as the car sped back to the city.

4

URBINO

Urbino, August 1510

At the entrance to the ducal palace the armed guard stopped the farmer and the boy and demanded to know their business. Enrico stuttered that he had come, with letters of introduction from Signor Giovanni Datini of Montecastelo, to deliver his son into the care of the court, as laid down in a letter from the duke himself. And here Enrico fumbled in his tattered tunic and fetched out the parchment sealed with the duke's insignia, an eagle surrounded by tongues of fire. The soldier could make no sense of the farmer's garbled story, but the seal was unmistakable. Shrugging his shoulders, the guard allowed the pair to enter and directed them to the stables, where the stableman would bring them to one of the household stewards.

The stableman took charge of the donkey and cart. He was polite, though Andrea detected his amusement and felt uncomfortable. They were led into the palace through a long tunnel-like entrance and were then ushered into the chief steward's office. The steward, a self-important man, took hold of Datini's letter of introduction and the one sent by the duke accepting Andrea into the court and perused them. 'Most strange,' was all the steward said, as he cast a puzzled look at the boy and his father. And then he blurted out, pointing to Enrico's right shoulder, 'Where in heaven's name are you bringing that?'

Enrico grinned, showing his two remaining teeth. 'The lamb is a gift for the duke's table.' And, as if to confirm the truth of Enrico's statement, the lamb bleated timidly. Enrico carried the animal wrapped around his neck, like a woollen muffler.

The steward's eyes narrowed to a frown. 'Come with me,' he said curtly.

He led the father and son across the courtyard. Andrea twisted his head this way and that to take in the subtlety of design and the craftsmanship in every detail of the building. At the far end of the courtyard Andrea caught a glimpse, through the open door, of the library – the greatest in all Italy, Menocchio had told him – and his heart beat with excitement. Somehow he, Andrea Doni, was going to be a part of this court. The steward led them up the vast staircase. He bid them wait and entered a room. He reappeared with the duke's chamberlain, who asked for the letters and read them with undisguised disbelief. The chamberlain bowed to Andrea with such a supercilious air that Andrea felt both shamed and angered at the same time.

Smiling broadly, the chamberlain spoke. 'Please step into the waiting room, gentlemen, and I will inform the duke that his guests have arrived.'

Andrea hoped that the ironic emphasis on the word 'guests' had been lost on his father. The chamberlain brought them into the first of the duke's private apartments and withdrew.

As they waited, Andrea marvelled at the wooden floor,

with its intricate, inlaid designs. He saw that the marble surround of the fireplace had leaping dolphins and zephyrs in full flight. Above his head the ceiling was stuccoed with mythical beasts of every kind. The walls were decorated with paintings and inlaid wood to create all kinds of clever illusions: there were *trompe l'œils* of an open window and a desk and chair. To Andrea, the room was disconcerting and disorientating. Then he and Enrico were summoned into the duke's study.

As they entered the room, he saw three men standing over a table, looking at a map spread before them. All were dressed in fine clothes and wore scent. Andrea noticed how clean and manicured their hands were. One wore a hat; the other two had shining and coiffured hair. All three men looked at the pair without offering a salutation or bidding them welcome.

Enrico was unnerved and addressed the most distinguished-looking of the gentlemen. 'Your Excellency, allow me to present to you my son, Andrea Doni of Montecastelo, who has come to learn from you,' and, when this met with no response, Enrico added, with an air of desperation, 'as you requested him to do.' The short speech cost Enrico such an evident effort of concentration that the three men exchanged looks of surprise and merriment.

The courtier addressed by Enrico responded with an exaggerated flourish. 'At your service, my good friend. I am Baldassare Castiglione, courtier to his excellency Francesco Maria della Rovere, Duke of Urbino.'

Every sound was rolled around the mouth of the courtier and savoured as one might savour a favourite taste. Castiglione gestured in the direction of the man to his right. The duke nodded, with a barely perceptible movement of his head and though he smiled Andrea thought his mouth tight and hard.

The duke remained silent and Enrico was forced to repeat his speech. His words having no apparent meaning to the duke, Enrico handed the documents to Castiglione to pass to him. The courtier, vain and fussy in the matter of his dress and appearance, handled the letters as if they were infected with pestilence. The duke glanced over them and raised his head to look at the boy. Andrea flushed under the duke's critical stare.

'Yes,' the duke said at last, with no hint of warmth in his voice, 'now I remember. So this is our scholar.'

Andrea looked at the duke, who held the boy's stare as he addressed Castiglione. 'Baldassare, this is a task I have in mind for you. You are to take this *enfant sauvage* and transform him into a courtier. You will have him taught the ways of the court and you will see to his musical and artistic training. You have twelve months and then we will review the progress you have made. If you succeed, you will be acclaimed as the greatest educator in Italy.'

Castiglione laughed. 'But which creature do you mean, Your Excellency? The old one, the young one or the one wrapped round the old one's shoulders?'

The third courtier laughed at Castiglione's joke and the duke smiled.

Enrico was too distracted to follow the conversation between the duke and his courtiers, but Andrea's ears burned with indignation. And, looking at his father, Andrea felt a protectiveness towards him that he had never known before. Growing bold in defence of Enrico, Andrea spoke. 'Your Excellency, my father has brought a gift for your table, a young lamb, which he would like to present to you in person, in return for your kindness in taking me into your academy.'

There was no response to this declaration but Andrea saw a look of mild panic pass over the faces of the three gentlemen at the prospect of handling a farm animal – arrayed as they were in the finery of the court. Andrea pressed home his advantage.

'Father,' he declared, 'give the lamb to the duke.' His father stepped forward, smiling guilelessly. The startled duke took a step backward, calling for his chamberlain, wishing to be rescued from this imbecile from the mountains who had a farm animal wrapped around his shoulders – and who treated his private apartment as if it were a butcher's shop! The chamberlain blustered in and the duke commanded him to bring the lamb and its owner to the kitchen.

'Take the boy too,' he ordered, 'and see that both are provided for after their long journey.'

Castiglione caught the laughter in Andrea's eyes and, for the first time since arriving at the palace, Andrea saw in the face of the courtier an acknowledgement of him as an intelligent human being. Castiglione bowed to the boy.

Andrea said, 'Sir, I am honoured that you will be my tutor and I will work to prove myself worthy of your attention.'

Castiglione was taken aback by the excellence of Andrea's speech. He smiled at Andrea.

'I look forward to making your further acquaintance,' he said and, with that, the chamberlain led Andrea and Enrico to the kitchens, where the cook greeted them and made them feel welcome.

Sitting in the kitchen drinking a glass of wine as the cook served some stew, Enrico found his confidence and began to brag of his son's genius. Andrea blushed but the cook received his father's remarks with such good humour that the boy relaxed and began to take his ease. The cook, Bernadetta, had a son and daughter, and her husband worked for the chief steward. The family had sleeping quarters next to the kitchen and Andrea asked if, for the first few nights, he might share their accommodation. Bernadetta agreed, provided, she added, that the chief steward had no objection, for he was in charge of all affairs relating to servants.

But, Andrea thought to himself, I am not a servant. I am a student and surely I will lodge, in time, with the other students.

But there was so much to take in that this thought passed from Andrea's mind.

After eating, Enrico rose to set out on the return journey. Andrea accompanied him to the stable to retrieve his cart. When the donkey had been harnessed, father and son took their leave of each other. The two embraced.

'Bless you, my boy,' Enrico said. But Andrea had no words and so turned from his father to start his new life in the palace of Urbino.

For the first few weeks Andrea lived between worlds in the palace. Bernadetta treated him like one of her own children, and he ran errands for her and helped her in the kitchen, listening to the gossip of the girls who came to help her. It was Bernadetta who, through the chief steward's office, arranged for clothes to be got for Andrea. And, for the first time, Andrea wore woollen hose with leather soles. He received three linen shirts, some breeches and a waistcoat. In his new clothes, Andrea felt more able to meet and converse with the inhabitants of the palace. For the palace was a veritable town, housing as many people as lived in Montecastelo and its neighbouring villages. And just as Menocchio spoke of the customers who called to the mill, Bernadetta spoke of those she fed with a forthright cynicism that combined shrewdness with pride: she maintained that, beneath all their finery, the courtiers had gullets like everyone else and were what they ate. Andrea laughed without saying anything unwise or foolish, for he was cautious by both nature and conviction.

Through Bernadetta, Andrea began to learn about the courtiers and their ways. Her talk was as spicy as the stews she prepared; when she spoke of this or that person, she peppered her remarks with casual, malicious barbs.

'Oh, Signor Castiglione is a fine gentlemen, with more learning in his head than any ten men together, which is why he is so careful and guards it against frost and cold and sun and wind. You will never see Signor Castiglione go without a hat. Now you must not think, young Andrea, that Castiglione is vain in the matter of his head, which, on top, is as bald as an egg.' And here Bernadetta let out a great, cheerful laugh. 'Ah, so much learning and so little sense. So it is with the great men of the world.'

But Bernadetta would not be drawn on the duke.

'The duke is not to be spoken of in jest,' is all she would venture, adding, 'Do not put yourself in the way of the duke.'

After a week in the company of Bernadetta and her family – and the servants who came in and out of the kitchens – Andrea grew familiar with the names and characters of the court and was less in awe of being amongst them. So when Baldassare Castiglione sought him out, Andrea was already much changed from the village boy who had arrived on a cart drawn by a donkey.

5

THE JOURNEY BACK

Prague 1995

The man and the boy stand at the viewing station overlooking the city. The day is clear and mild, though the breeze carries a chill that hints at the coming winter. The man points out some landmarks: the River Vltava, the tower at the Stone Bridge, the spire of Tyn Church, where the astronomer Tycho Brahe is laid to rest. The boy finds each landmark and smiles in triumph. In good spirits, they turn to begin their descent.

At the bottom of the steps they catch a tram. It drops them on the other side of the river, near Old Town Square. It is a weekday but there is still a sizeable number of tourists, who are, like Jacob Philip and his grandson, Ben, strolling around and browsing at the street traders' stalls. They buy a puppet from a vendor.

'It's the Golem,' Jacob says.

'The Golem, Grandad?'

'Don't you know about him?'

'No.'

'Oh dear,' Jacob sighs, shaking his head. 'The Golem,' he explains, 'was a creature made from clay by Rabbi Loew. The rabbi was a sorcerer.'

'A sorcerer!'

'Yes. Prague is a mysterious place, Benjamin, with a long history of magic. This Golem was a dim-witted, clumsy thing. But he protected the ghetto. And the rabbi inscribed "Emet" on the creature's forehead. Do you know your Hebrew?'

'No.'

'Shame on you! "Emet" means "truth". But if you rub out the "E", you are left with "met", which means "death"!' Jacob puts a finger to his mouth. 'Don't speak a word of this,' he warns. 'This is secret knowledge I am giving you, Benjamin. I hope you are listening.'

Ben nods solemnly and the two exchange a smile.

'You see,' Jacob resumes, taking the puppet in his hand to demonstrate, 'when the rabbi wanted to stop the Golem, he simply wiped out the letter "E" from the creature's forehead, like this.' He hands the puppet back.

'You're not asking me to believe this, Grandad?'

'You must always believe the truth.'

Ben looks at the puppet with a renewed sense of interest. 'This is the twentieth century, Grandad.'

'So much the worse,' Jacob replies, his face hardening.

Ben knows him well enough to fall silent.

They walk on. The boy tries on a jester's hat and makes his grandfather laugh when he jiggles his head and the bells tinkle merrily. They cross the square and make their way down a wide, tree-lined avenue. A group of tourists wearing prayer caps throng the pavement outside the oldest synagogue in the city. Jacob greets them in Hebrew.

'Shalom alekhem,' he says.

'Alekhem Shalom,' comes the reply.

Ben senses the tension in his grandfather, the hint of irascibility that alarms and attracts him. He waits.

'Here we are,' Jacob announces suddenly. 'This is the Pinkas Synagogue.' Ben looks around unmoved, not knowing what is expected of him.

Inside, the white walls are inscribed with the names of those killed by the Nazis. The family name in red, in large bold letters, the first names in black. Each name followed by a date of birth and a date of death. Ben goes on ahead, his eyes hardly registering the information. His grandfather follows more slowly, exchanging quiet words with those who read the names and pray. He stops before the surname 'Philip'. There are not many victims listed. He recognises none of them and yet he feels a tightening in his stomach. He coughs. A dry, tearless cough. Ben returns and Jacob takes his arm, leaning a little on him.

They come out into bright sunshine in the old cemetery. Headstones stand at bizarre angles, crowded one on top of the other. It seems smaller to Jacob than he remembered it. But memory, he understands, is like that. And he reminds himself that he is getting old. He raises his eyes to the expanse of blue above their heads. Ben asks him about the pebbles piled on the graves. The boy's voice breaks into his thoughts. He blinks and gives his grandson his full attention.

'In the old times, when our people wandered in the desert, there were no flowers to put on the graves of the loved ones. So our ancestors brought stones. Find some,' he says with sudden enthusiasm, 'and we'll leave them here, in memory of your great-grandparents.'

Ben hastens away to do his bidding. In his absence Jacob surveys the tiny cemetery. He was never here with his parents, yet he feels close to them. He reaches into an inside pocket for his notebook. He tears out a page and writes their names, 'Maria' and 'Benjamin', and a blessing. He folds the paper carefully and places it on a tomb, weighing it down with a small stone. Ben returns and places his pebbles beside it. His grandfather nods his approval.

'Good. Now there is one more place I want you to see before we go for lunch.'

At the far end of the cemetery they climb the steps of the ceremonial hall, a quaint, fairy-tale building. Inside is an exhibition of pictures and poems.

'These come from a town called Terezin,' Jacob says. 'It's not too far from here. It was used as a transit camp in the war.' He inspects the paintings and drawings. 'I was there,' he says, louder than he intended. 'I was there,' he repeats, as though the idea is too fantastic to be true. He reads a verse of poetry from among those displayed on the wall:

Who was toughened up before,
He'll survive these days.
But who was used to servants
Will sink into his grave.

Had he been toughened up before? Hardly. But he'd survived, somehow. And to be a survivor is important. He knows that. And to give witness is important. And he will.

They don't stay long. He doesn't want to grow morbid, so now they are walking again, in the fresh air, making for the Vltava. By the river, he settles himself on a bench and dozes in the sun. Nearby, Ben fishes with some local children, acting, Jacob thinks, like a child, in a way that the boy's smart, know-all parents would frown upon.

Jacob laughs to himself. He had wanted to protect his son, Ben's father, from the horror of the war and now he despises his innocence and his middle-class correctness.

Soon he will take Ben to Dresden. There he will tell him a little more. But for the moment he is content to snooze by the Vltava, lulled by the river's murmuring.

6

LIFE AT COURT

Urbino, 1510–11

When Castiglione came in search of Andrea, he noticed at once the change in the boy. The courtier bowed to his young charge.

'You look well in your new clothes. Now you will visit the barber and have your hair cut so that I might bring you into the company of the court one evening this week.'

'And when will I meet the other students, sir?' Andrea asked.

'Other students? There are no other students here.'

'But I came to study at the academy. To learn Latin and mathematics and to develop my skills as a painter. To work with the sons of the nobility and the sons of humble farmers, like myself.'

Castiglione, struck again by the quality of Andrea's speech and the earnestness of his nature, replied with gentle consideration, 'The days of an academy at Urbino are long gone. They passed with the death of Duke Federico de Montefeltre, grand-uncle of the present duke. He was a renowned scholar and warrior. But that is many years ago. You will be the only student. However, among the court there are the finest teachers.'

'The only student?' cried Andrea in dismay. 'But in the village . . . '

'In the village?' Castiglione asked, an ironic smile playing about his mouth, and the words died on Andrea's lips.

Castiglione saw the boy's misery and took pity on him and spoke with a new tenderness in his voice. 'You are the only student and that will make you special. And if you are as alert as your patron informs us, then you will thrive and become great.'

Andrea revived at the courtier's words. 'Well, sir, I am your student and am ready to commence my studies.'

'Then let us waste no time,' Castiglione declared, with an air of authority. 'Come, we will take a turn in the garden and I will begin your instruction.'

In Castiglione's company, Andrea felt himself to be a different person. Servants, who had spoken to him as one of their own as he sat in the kitchen with Bernadetta, now passed him with heads bowed and refused to catch his eye, though he wanted to greet them. And Castiglione moved as if the palace servants were not there. He neither greeted them nor expected them to greet him. They were invisible beings. Strolling in the formal garden, Castiglione began to expound on the nature of court life and the duty of the courtier.

'Know,' he began, 'that the first aim of the courtier is to be gracious in everything he does. It is of no consequence whether you are riding a horse, fighting a duel, combing your hair, or discoursing with a lady, you must exhibit graciousness. For it is in being gracious that you will win universal regard. And a courtier must always win regard.' Here Castiglione paused and looked gravely upon his pupil. Andrea, knowing that his tutor wanted an acknowledgement of these sententious remarks, nodded his head in affirmation.

'Good. This is the first lesson. Aim for universal regard through the graciousness of your conduct. You are young, Andrea, and fit and, no doubt, full of energy. But do not twist and cavort, or turn cartwheels, for these are the antics of peasants and clowns. Have regard now for your position as my student. By all means play tennis, for that will show your agility and dexterity, but avoid all vulgar display.'

Andrea sighed inwardly. Was it for this that he had left his home and parents, he wondered. And what, he asked himself, was 'tennis'?

Castiglione continued, 'Keep company with outstanding men – and here in Urbino are the most outstanding men of the age – and study them. Learn to carry yourself with ease, for it is vulgar to show too much effort or exertion. Strive to your utmost, but do not show the effort.'

Castiglione paused and smiled at Andrea as if he had revealed a great secret or admitted him into the golden circle. 'Be nonchalant and modest.'

That night as he lay on his mattress, hearing in the room next to his the animal sounds of Bernadetta and her husband, Andrea thought over the things Castiglione had told him. He needed time to arrange his own ideas, to sort out his confusions and objections. For, as Castiglione spoke to him, Andrea had felt an inexpressible frustration. His feelings, if not his thoughts, had prevented him from assenting to his master's words.

Now Andrea stumbled across his own beliefs and tried to formulate them into words. He spoke softly to himself, mindful not to wake the two children who slept in their bed in the opposite corner of the room.

'What Signor Castiglione teaches me is to act out a role, like the strolling players who visit our village. I am to act for the ladies and gentlemen of the court. But why must I act and disguise my efforts or my interests or angers? Should my father, labouring in the hot sun, pretend to be at ease? Should he disguise the ache in his back?'

And thinking of his father, Andrea felt the tug of home and wanted to be back where he belonged, among those whom he loved. For now, having left them, he had discovered his true feelings for them.

'And what,' he wondered aloud, 'would Menocchio make of Signor Castiglione's ideas?' Andrea laughed a little as he considered what Castiglione would make of Menocchio!

Andrea heard, in his head, Castiglione's voice. 'You must learn to write in the vernacular and in Latin. Be agreeable of face and graceful in manner. Learn to handle weapons like a gentleman. Feign ignorance rather than parade learning.'

His new master's voice was light and soft. He enunciated each word clearly, savouring every sound. His phrases were balanced and exact. He spoke without hesitation. Recalling Castiglione's lecture, for such it was, Andrea was impressed not by the thought or the sentiments it contained but by the tidiness of the intelligence that produced it. He smiled when he remembered the chaos of Menocchio's mind, for the miller spoke in violent fits of enthusiasm and many of his pronouncements ended in mid-sentence as fresh ideas forced themselves into his consciousness. But Andrea had no doubt that Menocchio was the better teacher, for he shared his enthusiasm and love of learning, whereas Castiglione used his learning to show off what he knew.

Andrea wondered if, beneath Castiglione's outward calm, there was a soul burning with passion. For the boy knew that *his* soul burnt with a passion to create. Furthermore he knew, in an instinctive way, that each person has to develop along the path of his or her genius and feelings and not in imitation of the ways of others. And whatever about the judgement of the court, Andrea knew that he would judge people by what lay within them and not by their clothes and manners.

Thinking this, he fell asleep. But his sleep was disturbed by dreams and visions. An angel, huge and fiery, sped over the land brandishing a sword. He crossed a river and the waters were set alight. And there was a plain where horses and men were entangled and striving against each other. Andrea awoke more than once in the night, feeling fearful and oppressed.

*

Andrea's education continued apace at court. Castiglione responded with enthusiasm to the duke's challenge to him to educate Andrea. Within a year a small group of courtiers gathered to crown him King of Educators, for Andrea was as accomplished a youth of fourteen years as it was possible to be. The glory, however, was not Castiglione's alone. Every member of the court took pride in Andrea's progress and education. The project, as it was termed by the courtiers, excited the curiosity of all. Many individuals offered to tutor Andrea in various arts, from fencing to reading the Latin poets. Each joked about his efforts on behalf of the poor lamb from the mountain.

Behind the jokes was a different story, for all who taught the boy loved their contact with him. Andrea was bright beyond his years and eager to learn, and he possessed such unaffected honesty and wonder that his company lightened the hearts of the courtiers. Through this boy, the members of the court rediscovered their own joy in learning. Andrea was loved because, in him, sophisticated men and women saw themselves as they had been in their innocent, youthful days.

With so much affectionate attention showered on him, Andrea grew in confidence. His natural flair for words deepened into a rich eloquence. Bernadetta did not allow him to lose his head, however. When he'd visit her in the kitchen she would greet him with an exclamation: 'Oh, my! How the lowly have been raised up in the sight of the Lord' or 'Doesn't our young shepherd smell sweet today?' Bernadetta's influence, and the letters he sent to Menocchio, kept Andrea in mind of the life he had left behind – a life where people struggled to keep body and soul together. Somewhere, between the world of toil and poverty and the world of ease and luxury, was the place where Andrea longed to be. At court he felt himself a stranger to both worlds.

Of course Andrea's chief tutor was Castiglione, who took him on as a page. Thus he had many opportunities to observe his master both at work and at play. Over the year, Andrea grew to know Castiglione without that knowledge turning to love. True, he did like and admire the courtier, for Castiglione was clever and charming, and Andrea marvelled at his power of argument and debate. But his master was manipulative and was driven by a desire to please the most powerful people in the court. He was the duke's closest adviser and, because Andrea was

Castiglione's page, the youth found himself close to the duke, an honour for which he cared little. For within a short time Andrea was to learn that, behind the smiles, the heart of the duke was as venomous as the fangs of a viper.

*

Andrea had been at court for over a year when the announcement was made of the forthcoming marriage between Bindo Gonzaga, a son of the Marquis of Mantua, and Elizabeth della Rovere, a niece of Francesco. The news put the court in a state of high excitement. The match had little to do with love and a great deal to do with politics, for the wedding would strengthen the ties between two states that were striving to maintain their independence from the great powers of France and Rome.

Francesco wished to spare no expense in staging the wedding. It was to be the most lavish affair seen in Urbino for many a day. As page to Castiglione, who had acted for the duke in the negotiation of a marriage settlement between the families, Andrea was busy running hither and thither for his master. He was involved in the preparations in other ways too. The Duchess Eleanor had requested that the court musician compose the music for a set of poems written for the occasion by Pietro Bembo. The music needed four voices, and Andrea, at the instigation of Castiglione, was auditioned and numbered among the court musicians and singers. So sweet was his singing that the bride-to-be, Elizabeth, developed a fondness for the youth and had him attend her whenever he was free to do so.

For his part, Andrea, then fifteen, felt the first rush of

love for Elizabeth and would, he believed, happily have died for her. In one of his lessons, Castiglione had spoken to his pupil of love and beauty. Andrea had not really paid attention to Castiglione's clever elaboration of the theme, but he did recall his master's assertion that the duty of the courtier was to see the angelic beauty in the woman he loved – a beauty that went beyond physical attraction and suggested the very light of heaven. In Elizabeth, Andrea saw that light. Above all else, he wished to express her radiance in painting. And soon he got his chance to do so.

At court, Timoteo Viti was retained as the duke's artist. Viti was a bear of a man, with wavy black hair streaked with silver. He wore a short, rough beard. Despite his great size, he was quiet and self-effacing. He knew both the extent of his talent and his limitations. He cared nothing for the fashionable idea of the painter as an artist imitating the work of the Creator. For Viti, painting was no different from other crafts. Each job presented a technical challenge and, like an engineer, Viti sought to find the most graceful solution to the problem. He took pride in his draughtsmanship and in his skill in mixing paints. But he was no showman. He carried out his commissions with as little fuss as possible.

Castiglione had asked the painter to take Andrea on as his assistant. There was no way of refusing this request, and Viti agreed to it with neither enthusiasm nor reluctance. At the time, Viti was working on a set of Stations of the Cross for a church in a neighbouring town. The duke was presenting the stations as a gift in return for the town's loyalty to him. Each station was to be painted on a wooden panel. When Andrea arrived, Viti had already completed the cartoons for most of the stations and had prepared the wooden panels to receive the paint.

With an economy of words rare for a member of court, Viti taught Andrea the rudiments of mixing pigments. He had no expectations of his student. Castiglione wanted the boy instructed in the skills of painting; he, Timoteo Viti, would instruct him. And then he would get on with his own work, mixing his own paint, while the youth kept out of his way.

At first Andrea's efforts were hopeless. The paint was too tacky or too runny. But little by little he began to learn the characteristics of each medium and pigment. Andrea's mind was careful and retentive. He did not repeat mistakes. He did not forget the lesson he had learned from previous experiments. Within a short time he was producing vibrant colours that were easy to handle.

Viti said little, but he noted Andrea's progress. And he invited him to make a preliminary sketch for the fourteenth station, *Jesus is Laid in the Tomb*. Andrea threw himself into the work. His sketch depicted the scene outside the tomb. Mary knelt to the left, the head of her son resting on her thighs. The body of Jesus sagged lifeless. But there was peace about the body, as if it had shaken off the violence of its death. Mary Magdalene rubbed oil upon the wounded feet, while a little to the right, the disciples huddled together in a group. The face of Peter showed despair. Within the folds of his garments Peter's body was slumped and tired. On a hill in the background could be seen the outline of three crosses.

Andrea worked on the sketch for a week. When it was completed, he showed it to the painter. Never had he worked with such determination and concentration on a piece before. He thought it was good but he could read nothing in the expression of Viti as the painter examined the finished drawing. At length, Viti spoke.

'Come, Andrea, I have work for you.'

That was all he said. But the tone of approval in his voice filled Andrea with the pleasure of success.

Viti worked on three panels at any one time. While he worked on the heads of the characters, he allowed Andrea to fill large areas of the composition. At first this was nearly all sky but, as the young man gained confidence in handling paint and in judging the surface upon which he worked, Viti allowed him to paint stone and some background. Andrea's touch was deft and sure. Occasionally he added a little feature of his own. A cloud in the sky. A bird in flight. A flower or plant in the foreground. Viti allowed these innovations to stand and he applauded Andrea's progress. For the final panel, Viti used Andrea's sketch and permitted his apprentice – for that was how Viti regarded him now – to trace the design on the panel and do most of the painting himself. Viti painted the face of each figure, but everything else was Andrea's.

One day, the duke summoned Viti to him. He wanted him to paint a large canvas, to be hung over the altar in the palace chapel. The painting would commemorate the marriage of Elizabeth and the marquis's son. Viti suggested a depiction of the Virgin greeting her cousin Elizabeth following the visit of Gabriel. The duke agreed, for he had no interest in painting and was happy for the artist to make the decision for him.

Viti returned to the studio, a self-contained unit in the quadrangle that housed the stables. Andrea was there, for he found the studio to be a haven from the hustle and bustle of the court. Andrea could be himself with Timoteo and need not worry whether his manner might fall short of the exacting standards required of a courtier. And Andrea and Timoteo had grown easy in each other's company. As soon as Viti entered, Andrea sensed his excitement.

'Come, we have some real painting to do, Andrea. A large canvas that will hang in the palace chapel. A work to celebrate the nuptials of Elizabeth della Rovere and Bindo Gonzaga.'

'What are we to paint, Timoteo?' Andrea enquired eagerly.

The Visitation of Mary to Elizabeth.'

Andrea burst out laughing.

The Visitation! This is a joke!'

But Timoteo was not smiling and he asked Andrea why he thought the idea so funny.

'Because,' Andrea replied, 'the Elizabeth of the Gospels is an old woman. Will you paint an old woman to represent the duke's niece? On her wedding day is Elizabeth to gaze upon the face of a woman, bearing her name, who is stricken with age?'

Timoteo frowned. At length he said, 'But the painting is not intended as a portrait of Elizabeth della Rovere.' And, smiling, he added, 'Besides, in our version, we can make the Elizabeth of the Gospels into a *young* old woman.'

Andrea laughed. 'A very young old woman,' he said.

Undeterred by Andrea's scepticism, Viti began to think out loud, planning preliminary sketches for his *Visitation*. And because the work was intended for Elizabeth's wedding, Andrea asked if he too might prepare some sketches on the theme. Viti agreed, and Andrea, in high good spirits, set off to find Castiglione.

Elizabeth della Rovere was young and vivacious, and around her gathered the young ladies of the court. As her marriage approached, she thought it wise to confine her evening entertainment to female company. With a select group of friends, she read poetry and spoke of marriage and love. If Andrea was not required by Castiglione, Elizabeth requested him to attend her. For these evenings, the youth took special care with his appearance and even made use of a little of Castiglione's fragrances. He ran and fetched for his lady, or sang a song, or recited poems which she had asked him to memorise. Andrea served Elizabeth as if his very life depended upon it. The poems that she read spoke his heart. Some lines of Catullus burned themselves into his mind:

I hate and I love. Why? You may ask but
It defeats me. I feel it done to me, and ache.

Through Elizabeth's circle, Andrea heard the poetry of Ovid – his skittish love poems and the poems of sorrow and separation he wrote while in exile:

My letter comes to you in another's hand,
For I have lain ill in the remotest region
Of an unknown land,
Doubting if I'd ever be well again.

You, my beloved, so far away,
I talk to every day.
Your name only I recite,
For without you, there is no night
Or day, or week or month or year.

Ovid's words expressed Andrea's feelings for Elizabeth, the bride-to-be. And feeling made him bold, for he begged her to allow him to draw her portrait as she sat conversing with her friends. Laughing, Elizabeth consented, and Andrea determined to channel his feelings into the work, for he remembered Castiglione's remark that the love befitting a courtier brings with it neither shame nor displeasure.

Andrea's portrait-sketch was a masterpiece. Not only did he capture the shape of Elizabeth's face but he knew how to highlight its beauty. His portrait caught the clear line of chin and jaw, the high cheekbones and the luminosity of her eyes. But it was Andrea's drawing of her mouth, with its sweet, moist, full lips, that revealed most clearly that the eye of the artist was filled with desire and love. Elizabeth begged him to give her the portrait, but he insisted that it was not quite complete and managed to hold on to it until it was forgotten. But the face did not stay hidden, for when Viti's painting of *The Visitation* was completed, it was noted that the angel, who hovered above the two women as they embraced, had a face of exquisite beauty. And more than a few observers thought the face familiar but could not place it. Elizabeth, however, knew the face to be her own, idealised as an angel, and she saw the love that brought the face to life even as it gazed down upon her as she made her marriage vows.

*

Timoteo was pleased with the work, and with Andrea's contribution to it. His pleasure was doubled when Raphael, whose father had been the court painter at Urbino, came to the workshop a few days before the wedding and praised *The Visitation*.

Viti credited the success of the painting to his talented helper and pointed out the areas of the canvas that had been completed by his young apprentice. Raphael, young and smiling, seemed no more than politely interested in Viti's account of the painting and its composition. True, he did smile when the older man showed him how he had overcome the problem of Elizabeth's age by having her turn away from the spectator to greet her young cousin. But Andrea did not anticipate what would happen next: just days later he was summoned and offered a position in Raphael's studio in Rome.

The youth was amazed and flattered by the offer, but he was also frightened by the prospect of Rome. Besides, he felt at home in Urbino and loved Timoteo Viti. So he declined the invitation.

But all this occurred in the days before the murder of Cardinal Giulio Chesi, in the court of Urbino – the knowledge of which event Andrea possessed but dared not reveal.

7

THE MADONNA

Prague, 1995

On the train to Dresden Jacob begins his story.

'After Father disappeared, Mother and I moved to Dresden.'

'Why Dresden?'

'Because it was an open city. It had no military importance, so people were free to come and go. And because of Raphael.'

'Raphael? As in Leonardo and Donatello – the painter?'

'Yes.'

'But what has Raphael got to do with Dresden and you going there?'

Grandfather Jacob laughs. 'Be patient, Benjamin. My mother came from Italy. You knew that?'

Ben nods.

'Well, she came from the north, from Piacenza. We're going to visit there in a few days. And it was for this city, my mother's city, that Raphael painted one of his most beautiful paintings.'

Ben interrupts. 'Grandad, you're not going to give me a straight answer, are you?'

'Of course not! Where's the pleasure in that? You must

wait a little and let the story unfold. Let the storyteller enjoy himself!'

Ben affects a groan. Jacob chuckles.

'When we arrived from Berlin, mother and I went wandering in our new city. We were free for the first time in years to walk where we pleased. How lovely that was! We strolled here and there, following streets where they led. One day, quite by chance, we came across the art gallery, the Gallery of Old Masters. Mother was really excited. You see, *The Sistine Madonna* hangs there.'

'You're losing me, Grandad.'

'*The Sistine Madonna* is the painting by Raphael.'

'But I thought you said he painted it for Pizza . . . '

'"Piacenza". He did, but it was sold to Dresden. And here was mother, from Piacenza, in Dresden, about to view her favourite painting! Now, do you understand?'

'Yeah,' Ben says doubtfully.

'Good.'

Jacob's thoughts drift away. He doesn't really have a personal history, an autobiography, in the way most people have. Instead, there are fragments, brilliantly illuminated – like this one of his mother in the gallery – and then dark shadows. And the fragments and shadows concern a boy who bears his name, a boy to whom he feels, at times, no more than the faintest connection.

'So what happened then,' Ben prompts, 'in the gallery?'

'We found the painting, and mother was beside herself with excitement. And she told me a story. A strange little story. When she was a young girl, she went to Mass every Sunday in the Church of San Sisto, where Raphael's Madonna hangs above the high altar. But she took no notice of it – it was just a painting. One Sunday, however, a miracle happened. As she was sitting there in the church, she saw faces emerge from the clouds. She told me that she saw, all around the edge of the canvas, the faces of little children appearing, taking shape before her very eyes! Some were smiling, but others were crying, and they seemed crowded together. And she was frightened.'

'But what did she mean, Grandad, about faces appearing?'

'I don't think she understood it very well herself. Her father hushed her and would not listen. So she sat there for twenty minutes, terrified of those shadowy appearances. And she didn't believe her father when, afterwards, he told her that the faces had always been there, hovering in the background of the painting. And she didn't believe him when he said they were the faces of heaven's angels. Mother insisted that the faces were those of little children, some smiling, some sad, some frightened. "Lost children" is how she described them. Anyway, mother never missed a Sunday Mass in San Sisto after that. And for years she'd go just to sit before the Madonna.

'So you can understand how eager she was when we entered the Gallery of Old Masters. For the really extraordinary thing is that the painting in Piacenza is only a copy. The original hangs in Dresden, and has done so for hundreds of years.

'I'll never forget mother on that day. She was reckless, almost crazy. You know how quiet and churchlike galleries are. But here was mother shouting at the top of her voice. The things she said were half mad!'

'What kind of things,' Ben asks.

'Well, for one, she closed her eyes and said that she could see the Madonna better with them like that. And then she stood as close to the painting as possible and shouted out, 'Ah, what a beautiful painting! Look, look,

Jacob! Look at the feet of the Virgin! Look!"

'Did you pretend you didn't know her?'

'Oh, I was embarrassed by her antics but I think I was proud of her, too.'

Jacob smiles to himself. He remembers the awkward feelings of his younger self, how he had looked around him, hoping that no one was there to witness his mother's behaviour. Fortunately, there was no one about, only a guard who looked through them as though they were invisible.

'So what did you do?'

'I led mother to a seat in the centre of the room and urged her to calm down. And she did. But then she looked at that painting with such longing that I felt as though she had left me. I sat really close to her and put my head on her shoulder. But she was too lost in the painting to take any notice of me.'

In the Natural History Museum in Dublin, where Jacob and Ben often go, many of the display cases are hidden beneath leather covers. You raise the flap to view the contents. It brings an excitement to the otherwise stale pleasure of viewing museum exhibits. Recalling his mother before the Sistine Madonna is, for Jacob, like raising a cover on his past or unwrapping a family heirloom.

'I remember,' Jacob continues, 'turning to the painting. I had been in Piacenza as a little boy, but I had no recollection of the church or of this Madonna stepping towards me on a bank of white clouds. Beneath her were two cherubs. I smiled at those two. And then suddenly, out of the blue, a wonderful thought filled my mind and took hold of it. The little angel, the one with his finger to his mouth, was my guardian, my soul brother.' Jacob continues before Ben can interrupt. 'I was delighted, more than delighted, because it felt so good, so comforting to have a guardian angel. And I named him Gabriel.'

Ben looks doubtfully at his grandfather.

'Well,' Jacob exclaims, 'don't you have a guardian angel?'

'No, of course not,' the boy replies, laughing at the idea.

'Oh, you do. You aren't aware of him, that's all.'

'Oh come on, Grandad!'

'It's true, Benjamin. I'm convinced that it was my angel who helped me to survive the war. And I believe he still watches over me. Over us.'

8

A WEDDING

Urbino, Autumn 1511

Andrea dressed carefully on the morning of the wedding. 'Today,' he thought, 'is the most important day of my life. Today I will sing for Elizabeth, for Raphael and for the Holy Father.'

The arrival of an ambassador from Rome with the news that Pope Julius had decided to come to Urbino to celebrate the nuptial mass of Elizabeth della Rovere and Bindo Gonzaga caused an elated panic among the court. Castiglione, chief adviser to the duke, met the ambassador to agree on protocol and discuss every aspect of the Pontiff's stay in Urbino, down to the food he would eat and the manner in which it was to be served. And now the great day was at hand.

Andrea put on his new livery. He looked at himself in the mirror, pinning his soft, red velvet hat to the back of his head. He arranged his hair, which he had brushed till it gleamed and then curled, so that it fell in ringlets about his shoulders. Andrea admired his white shirt. Twisting himself, he turned to view the back of his yellow tunic.

'Yes,' he said aloud, 'very elegant.'

Andrea was pleased, for the tunic showed off his slender waist. Even the particoloured hose in red and yellow struck the right note of pageantry. The red felt boots did not inspire his confidence but Signor Castiglione had insisted on them so they had to be borne. But Andrea was not going to let the boots spoil his day. He splashed a little rose-water on a handkerchief and dabbed it on the back of his neck. He inhaled the perfume and sighed, like any true lover. From the dressing table he took a small silver ring and placed it on the third finger of his right hand. The ring was a gift from Elizabeth, in thanksgiving for his dedicated service to her. It was his most prized possession.

He glanced once more in the mirror. It was hard to believe that in twelve months he had changed from an ignorant peasant boy into this grand member of the court of Urbino. He wondered what his parents, who were coming to the town for the celebrations, would think of him. He wasn't sure. Looking at himself through their eyes, Andrea felt less confident of the figure he cut. Today, however, was not a day for misgivings, it was a day to venture forth boldly. And, he reminded himself, he would not see his parents till after dark, when Signor Castiglione released him from his duties. Andrea took a final look at himself in the mirror and strode with purpose to his master's room.

Castiglione was flustered. The procession bringing the Pope and his entourage was nearly at the gates of the palace. He shouted instructions and cancelled them and bustled back and forth to no real purpose. For the first time since making his acquaintance, Andrea realised that his master was nervous and excited. They hurried to take their position in the welcoming party.

their position in the welcoming party.

A mounted escort of Swiss guards, their polished breastplates shining in the sun, led the way. Drummers beat a marching rhythm. A colour party carried the banners of the della Rovere family and the Papal flags. All was colour, noise and excitement. Banners of red silk with golden stars surrounded Julius as, flanked by his personal guard, he approached the town mounted on a white stallion. To Andrea's surprise, the Pope's dress was simple, without the trappings of wealth and power that he saw in the dress of the high-ranking clergy who came, from time to time, to the ducal palace. He wore a white surplice and cape, with the letters 'IHS' embroidered on it in golden thread. His hands were uncovered. True, on six of his slender fingers he wore rings, but these included the white diamond of faith, the green emerald of hope and the red ruby of charity.

The crowd cheered the Holy Father to the echo and he acknowledged them by giving his blessing as he rode past. Behind him, the procession stretched away as far as the eye could see: soldiers, supply wagons and a caravan of carriages bearing those Vatican officials and courtiers who were too old or overweight to ride a horse. The path to the palace was strewn with flowers. A fanfare of trumpets announced the arrival of the della Rovere Pontiff to the court of Urbino.

On a specially erected platform, which had been festooned and painted in gay colours, the duke, Francesco della Rovere, and a select band of courtiers stood to greet the Pope. Andrea, positioned near Castiglione, could see the anxiety in the duke's face. A year earlier, Francesco had been in command of a Papal force as it sought to keep the city of Bologna from falling into the hands of the French. But the Bolognese had grown restless under Papal authority and, amid confusion and rumours of armed revolt, Francesco had ordered a retreat, whereupon the French had seized the city.

To this day, the duke believed that the unrest in the city had been fomented by a group of cardinals. For the family had enemies – other powerful families, like the Medicis of Florence – who resented the power and influence that the papacy conferred upon Julius and his relatives. After the fiasco, the disgraced duke had stabbed Cardinal Francesco Alidosi to death, suspecting him of treason. The duke had stood trial for murder but had been acquitted. Thereafter, relations between Julius and himself had been strained. The Pontiff did not like failure, and his nephew had failed. Francesco knew that the Pope's attendance at the wedding was a sign of reconciliation and forgiveness. With all his heart, he wanted the visit to be successful.

And now the Pontiff was before him. The stallion was led to the platform. From the ceremonial saddle Julius stepped nimbly down onto firm ground. Francesco knelt before him and bowed his head in submission. Julius laid his hands upon his nephew and blessed him. Then Francesco raised his head to kiss the Papal ring. Paris de Grasis, the Vatican's Master of Protocol, signalled to Francesco to rise and the duke embraced the Pontiff, as nephew to uncle. Andrea felt a lump in his throat as he watched the Duke of Urbino embrace the Pope of Rome. The crowd cheered and all was well with the world. Then Francesco introduced the leading members of his court to Julius. As each one knelt to kiss his hand, Andrea observed the Vicar of Christ.

Julius was tall and thin, with a gaunt face and a severe expression. His long, fine beard gave him a saintly appearance. And though he was stooped and his eyes were sunken in his head, power emanated from him. The Pontiff looked into the distance, unsmiling. Of the dignitaries on the platform, Raphael alone seemed at ease. He knelt to kiss the Pope's ring and then rose, chatting with the easy, natural charm that Andrea so admired. And Julius responded to him in kind. It was clear that the Pope liked and trusted the painter. Andrea could not take his eyes from the Pontiff. He was fascinated and mesmerised by him.

The introductions over, the procession moved inside the palace. The crowds cheered, the sun shone and the day got off to a glorious beginning.

*

The Latin of the nuptial mass recited by Julius in a clear, strong voice filled the ducal chapel. Observing him from the choir, Andrea thought the Holy Father celebrated the mass as if he were alone before God. The congregation, including Elizabeth and her bridegroom, Bindo Gonzaga, held themselves in reverent stillness as Julius delivered the sacred words. At the Communion, the Pope placed the host on the tongues of the bride and groom and offered the chalice to them. Then, as the cardinals, who con-celebrated the Mass, administered the Eucharist to the congregation, Julius sat and listened to the choir. It seemed to Andrea that the Holy Father was transported by the music, for he closed his eyes and leant towards it, still and rapt. In the quiet of the church, with the Pope in attendance, and watched over by an angel who bore the face of his beloved Elizabeth, Andrea felt the full force of the sweet, solemn music he sang.

After the reverence and solemnity of the Mass, the celebration of the wedding burst out into the sunny airiness of the great courtyard, which was bedecked with flags and bunting. As the wedding party emerged into the sunshine, word passed from within the palace to those thronged outside. Immediately a great shout of good-humoured cheering was raised. Local bands of musicians struck up their festive tunes. The carnival was under way. In the piazza before the palace, sturdy tables were laid with bread, oil and casks of wine. Servants, aided by members of the palace guard, distributed the food. The revellers, among them Andrea's parents, ate, joked and danced. Hawkers set up their stalls and sold their wares. The fun was boisterous and energetic. Andrea imagined his mother and father among the throng. It made him sad to think of them, for he knew that it was more than the walls of the palace that lay between them and him.

Inside, the court sat down to an elaborate feast. Julius sat at the centre of the high table. His chair was on a small dais, which raised him above the other guests. He was attended by his personal servant. The master of protocol hovered close by, as did the Pope's physician. The Papal bodyguard scrutinised all who passed close to the Pontiff. Francesco and his wife, Eleanora, shared the table with the Marquis and Marquesa of Mantua and the wedding couple. Three lines of tables, covered in white cloth and laid with silver cutlery and beakers, ran the length of the courtyard.

To the accompaniment of music and singing, the feast

was served. From his place among the minstrels, Andrea observed it all. When the guests seated themselves and the warm towels had been passed among them, the procession of food and wine began. (It was rumoured in the town that Francesco had hired thirty cooks to prepare the banquet, though Bernadetta insisted that they worked to her commands!) The dishes were paraded around the courtyard. The most elaborate were placed before the bride and groom, then the food was assembled on serving tables and portions brought to each guest. The duke sat smugly, delighting in the display of his wealth. Elizabeth looked beautiful. She chatted, and smiled at all around her. Andrea felt the muscles of his heart constrict and knew the pain of love.

The banquet was splendid. The diners ate and laughed. The musicians played. The singers sang. The servants brought more plates of food and refilled the wine glasses. Wine flowed. There were speeches and applause, and then the entertainers appeared: jugglers, acrobats and jesters.

Before the dancing began, hundreds of white doves were released into the air. Andrea watched them circle and wheel, rising higher and higher. When darkness descended and the torches were lit, the master of cere-monies announced the fireworks spectacular. At his command, thirty Catherine wheels within the palace, and the same number outside, were lit and fountains of light were sent whirring through the night air. There were excited 'ooh's and 'aah's from the crowds, followed by applause and cheering. Firecrackers exploded. Torches gave off coloured smoke. In rapid succession, clusters of stars exploded in the sky. The night was lit by bursts of colour. To Andrea it seemed as if a firestorm was raging in the sky. Perhaps, indeed, the angels in heaven were waging war. The gold and crimson hue of the sky made him gasp in astonishment, yet, as he watched the sparks fall earthwards and burn themselves out, he was possessed by an unshakeable sadness.

The festivities continued. The courtiers moved indoors to the great hall. There was poetry and singing. Time flew, so that it was after midnight when Andrea made his way to the palace entrance to meet his parents. All the inns in Urbino were full and many of the wealthy lords in the surrounding countryside had been urged to extend their hospitality to guests and officials coming to the wedding. Andrea had arranged with Bernadetta for his mother and father to bed down in one of the two rooms assigned to her family as living quarters.

Although his parents were flushed with the excitement of the day, a hesitant silence fell over them when they came face to face with their son. The fashionable livery that had pleased Andrea that morning was now an embarrassment, as were his refined manners and cultured way of talking. His mother treated him as a fine gentleman. He wanted to protest that he was the same Andrea who had left Montecastelo but, in his heart of hearts, he knew this was not the case. So it was a subdued little party that made its way to the kitchen to find the lodgings. As he fell asleep, Andrea was beset by an unendurable sense of loss: the loss of both Elizabeth and his family.

9

FRANZ HELLER

Dresden, 1944

Franz Heller sat at his writing desk. A candelabra with seven candles cast light on the work area. A glass of white wine stood poured. He raised it to his lips and sipped, savouring the sweetness of the liquid. He let the wine wash around his palate and swallowed it without hurry. He replaced the glass and closed his eyes.

He pictured the emperor, Rudolf, standing at a window in the upper floors of the castle, the *hrad*, a spyglass, to his eye, surveying the sleeping city and the dark water below. The night was damp. A mist hung on the river. The Vltava's breath drifted towards the wakeful emperor. He withdrew a little, fearing the humours and poisons that rose from the murky depths.

His spyglass fastened on a hurrying figure, a night-walker, crossing the stone bridge. It gave him a thrill to stand invisible, watching the comings and goings of the night. The figure was that of a woman, a shawl thrown over her head. The hidden observer could not see her face, but he imagined it – sallow-skinned and fine, the kind of face that he admired.

Heller opened his eyes. He straightened the cuffs of

his smoking jacket, stretched his legs and eased the tension from his back and shoulders. Quince, his Abyssinian cat, asleep on his lap, purred in complaint at this disturbance. He stroked her. He thought of Rudolf's fondness for cats and once again his imagination returned to the castle above the city. His fascination with His Imperial Majesty Rudolf II, Holy Roman Emperor, madman, collector, genius, who died in 1612, a few days after the death of his favourite lion, was insatiable. Heller despised the emperor's gullibility and his childish fears. But he shared his love of collecting and he too knew the pleasure of watching, unobserved, the world pass by.

Everywhere Heller went he cast sly glances at those around him. On a tram he stole looks at the women in the carriage: their faces, their hands, the way their garments fell, the suggestion of their female form. Sometimes he was moved to secret, silent admiration; at other times an unsuspecting woman, travelling home to her husband and family, moved him to loathing. Occasionally, without expectation, Heller was thrown off balance by a woman's beauty: a movement of the head, a gesture of the hand, a crossing of legs. Then he looked away, in confusion, fearing the emotions he experienced.

And then there were the women he encountered for whom he felt an inexplicable tenderness. Yesterday in the gallery, for example. That dark-skinned woman, before the Sistine Madonna, with the boy. He had stepped into an adjoining room and watched her. The memory of her before Raphael's masterpiece moved him beyond words. She was still in his mind as he put pen to paper and wrote:

Holding the gold candelabra aloft, the emperor made his way through the winding corridors high above the city. Shadows danced on the walls as he moved through the labyrinth. Their presence thrilled and frightened him. From time to time he thought that he himself was no more than a shadow, a ghostly presence haunting the castle. A form without substance, face or identity.

The only sounds were those he himself made: the swish of his dark cloak, his footfall. Rudolf imagined that his journey to the treasure rooms had an analogue below in the city, as another solitary wanderer made his way through the alleyways and ramshackle houses of the ghetto. A lonely soul seeking comfort.

And then Rudolf was possessed of a fanciful idea which brought a faint smile to his features. All the nocturnal wanderers, himself included, were puppets in a play devised by the Divine puppet master. Or they were automata set in motion by a clever clockmaker – a collection of cogwheels and levers which moved with the stiffness of things mechanical. Again he allowed a smile to soften his features. Indeed, he felt a stiffness in his joints, the stiffness of age. And immediately thoughts of the tiny cemetery in the ghetto came to mind, where the dead were laid in layers one on top of the other. Rudolf's face puckered and twitched as the distressing thought of mortality wormed its way, yet again, into his mind, though he strove to keep it at bay.

Heller stopped writing. He sipped his wine. With the index finger of his left hand he smoothed the hairs of his moustache and stroked his upper lip before perusing what he had written. As he reread his work he marvelled at how Rudolf's morbidness had found its way onto the page. He had wanted to write of the emperor's private collection, yet it was death and the Jewish cemetery that had come from his pen.

Why? Perhaps because, as a boy, he'd visited the cemetery with his family. He had been too young – six or seven – to appreciate it. But now he could picture it clearly. The lime trees with their white blossoms. The chaos of headstones, crowded and close together, twisted at strange, disconcerting angles, as if the dead heaved and pushed at night, trying to escape from the narrow, suffocating spaces in which they lay confined.

Heller regarded his own apartment, with the heavy blackout curtains and his collection silent on the shelves. It had the air of a mausoleum. He laughed, mocking his thoughts, but they would not be banished. He was irritated by his foolishness. Time to get back to Rudolf in his castle. It was best to avoid introspection. The mind was a dark and murky place.

*

Franz Heller quit his desk promptly at half past five. A number of his fellow workers were chatting amiably and he bid them 'Good evening' as he passed. 'Goodbye, Herr Heller,' a male colleague called out with mock formality, and the others laughed. Heller did not look back.

'Heil Hitler,' the guard said as he left the ministry building, and Heller returned the salutation. In this manner, another ordered day was concluded, and Franz Heller hastened home through the streets of Dresden.

At forty-seven, he had the mien of a man twenty years his senior. His dress was sombre, like an undertaker's, and his conversation distant and polite. In truth, his colleagues regarded him as a harmless eccentric. They joked about his fastidious nature and his passion for neatness and exactitude. His secretive manner was attributed to his acute shyness. The fact that he was a bachelor was offered as an explanation for his mild hypochondria. With no one to take care of, so the argument went, Heller lavished all his attention upon himself.

The conversation in the office often turned, with amusement, to the obsessive traits in his personality. What his co-workers did not know – though they might have guessed – was that their associate was every bit as fanatical in his domestic obsessions as he was in his workplace ones. There was, for example, the compulsive economising – a fear of spending his money on what he termed 'non-productive purposes'. True, he drank expensive wine and smoked the occasional cigar, and there were the treats he bought for himself – a fine-cut crystal glass or a silver knife and fork – but these luxuries were paid for by a rigorous discipline in his daily budget.

It was his obsession with minutiae, however, that dominated Heller's life. In his work, this expressed itself in an ambition to fill every page of his ledger with the maximum number of lines, in the smallest possible writing. Outside his work, he collected shells, fossils and semi-precious stones. He was continuously on the lookout for minute, perfect specimens. His sizeable collection of these objects was the main feature of his apartment. The stones were lovingly displayed on glass shelves against a mirror backing so that each item could be viewed from every possible angle.

Alone in his apartment except for his cat, Franz Heller spent his feeling upon his worthless collection of tiny, lifeless objects. He held them in his hand and examined them tenderly under his magnifying glass. He recited their names aloud as a lover calls out the name of his beloved. He devised an elaborate taxonomy, classifying objects according to their physical characteristics and the pleasure he derived from their contemplation. In a large, leather-bound notebook he listed every item in his possession. Headings and subheadings were inscribed in coloured ink so that the pages had the appearance of a medieval manuscript. For Heller, there was an unceasing fascination in looking at and handling his treasures. Not for him the museum aridity of display cases. No, he loved his children, as he called them. Each and every one. Each piece spoke to a different mood in him. Unlike people, they never failed him. They accepted him for what he was. It was to them that he hastened home through the crepuscular light of the city.

His apartment was a refuge, for Heller did not feel at home in Germany or in the age in which he lived. The modern sensibility, as he termed it, found no echo in his soul. No, he despised the word 'modern'.

Some years earlier, at the prompting of his SS superior, he had attended an art exhibition organised by the Nazi Party to show the sordidness of the modern imagination. The exhibition featured the work of celebrated painters: Pablo Picasso, Paul Klee, Wassily Kandinsky. Heller hated everything he saw. What, he wondered, did these artists know of beauty? In a notebook of quotations he recorded with approval the Führer's sentiment that 'Art must be the messenger of noble and beautiful things, of all that is natural and healthy.' There was too much ugliness and corruption in the art of the modern painters.

But there was more to Heller's unhappiness than his feeling of displacement. There was fear. Before the Nazis came to power, he had strolled freely through the wide streets of Munich. He loved the city. He loved the anonymity that it conferred on him. On Saturday afternoons he'd take to the streets, stopping to drink coffee, looking at theatre posters or browsing at shop stalls.

And then the Brownshirts appeared on the streets and their presence inhibited his aimless strolling. For Heller feared to draw attention to himself in any way. On the streets, in the open, with Brownshirts everywhere, he felt exposed, vulnerable.

So Heller lost the pleasure of private meditation in the open spaces of Munich. He was driven indoors. His confinement was, at first, unbearable. Deprived of a city, Heller began, gradually, to create one in his mind. He read all that he could find on Prague, a place he had visited as a child, and began to write about it – and about the ghosts that haunted its ancient streets. Down Prague's labyrinth of alleyways his mind wandered. Magical Prague, capital of the Holy Roman Empire, presided over by the mad emperor, Rudolf. This was the city that seized hold of Heller, the city he invented in recompense for the one that had been taken from him. Prague of the alchemists and astrologers, the astronomers and the artists. The city of dreams and delusions, the city of magical transformations, where men, in secret laboratories, sought the elixir of life and the stone that would turn base metals into gold. In dreams, Heller was summoned before Emperor Rudolf and invited to observe the movement of the heavenly bodies and read the future in them. As his physical world contracted, Franz Heller's imagination grew bold and expansive.

And then he took to the art galleries. At first he wandered without purpose but, by degrees, he became systematic in his viewing of paintings. Holidays were spent travelling to galleries wherever he thought it safe to do so. He kept a note of the works he observed, and gradually his notes took the form of fragments, epigrams, aphorisms. But he would not respond to a painting without first consulting some authority. He was too timid to trust his own eyes or his own mind, too used to following orders and curtailing his opinions, too accustomed to saying what he felt his superiors wanted to hear. So he read art critics and copied out the statements he admired. He had a notebook of quotations, interspersed with his own rules for art, which he entitled his 'Little Book of Aphorisms'.

In the government department where he worked, Heller held himself aloof from his fellow workers. True, as his colleagues suggested, this was done partly out of a natural shyness. But it was mainly down to fear.

When the Nazis had come to power, civil servants were obliged to establish their Aryan identity. This require-ment threw up a new class of family researchers, who provided proof of German ancestry. And it threw up a legion of forgers, one of whom provided Heller with the documents he needed, for he was not the person he claimed to be.

In 1917 he had left his native Ukraine, fleeing from the persecution of Russian forces. He had made it to Germany, where he had assumed the name 'Heller' and started a new life. When, in 1935, the documents arrived and his position in the civil service was secure, he requested a transfer to Dresden. He could not bear the thought that the man he had paid to forge the documents would have it in his power to blackmail him. Moving away from Munich lessened that fear but the fear itself did not leave him. Indeed, it governed his life.

In Dresden, Heller worked for the Directorate of Railways. From 1939 onwards his work involved, among other things, making deportation schedules and timetabling trains to and from the camps at Buchenwald and Rehmsdorf. Later, as the war progressed, the schedules were for trains transporting evacuees east to Auschwitz. This work was carried out under the watchful eye of an SS commandant.

Heller was meticulous in his job. He prided himself on the accuracy of his lists and the neatness of his hand. He formed each letter or figure with care. He was conscious of his hand moving on the page as he made upstrokes and downstrokes. He loved the curving form of the 'o' and the 's'. Memos written to superiors were miniature works of art. He thought of timetabling and cross-referencing as a kind of pure mathematics. He had none of the curiosity or imagination needed to turn lists, facts and figures into human reality – or rather, he had trained himself to suppress these impulses. A deportation train was an 'x' to be shunted between an 'a' and a 'b'. The passengers, the prisoners, were cargo.

After six years of arranging the transport of 'cargo', he had assisted in the removal of hundreds of thousands of Jews to Poland. But this thought was not allowed to intrude into Heller's consciousness. He maintained the detachment and neutrality of the scientific observer.

Another part of his job was to keep a record of the Jews arrested in Dresden: Name. Age. Sex. Personal possessions seized and confiscated. Destination. In the case of a householder, a list was made of the property confiscated by the state. The value of seized goods was estimated and tallied. Heller compiled these inventories with infinite patience. Everything was recorded, ordered and filed. He liked to think of himself as following in the tradition of Tycho Brahe, the Danish astronomer. Brahe's careful measurements of the stars and planets laid the basis for a new understanding of the universe. Heller reasoned that the accumulation of countless, accurate lists formed, when regarded in the proper light, a work of pleasing harmony. A work of art of sorts.

As in all conversations with the self, Heller did not tell the full story. The care and attention to detail evident in his work, highly valued as it was by the SS, was born of guilt, for deep down – so deep that he never acknowledged it – he understood the fate of the evacuees moved by him from place to place and, if nowhere else then at least in his work, each name was recorded and given its place in the grand scheme of creation and destruction. Each name was recorded for posterity.

*

In Dresden there were fewer art galleries than in Munich so Heller found himself, again and again, in the Gallery of Old Masters. And, more often than not, his visit to the gallery concluded with a viewing of Raphael's *Madonna*. Creature of habit that he was, Heller liked to view the painting from the same spot on each occasion.

One day, in July 1944, he discovered that his favourite seat was occupied by a young boy. He was irked by this, believing that his love for the painting gave him exclusive rights to it. He sat beside the boy, hoping that the child would relinquish the seat. But he didn't. For Jacob came to the gallery more and more often. He came to speak with his guardian angel, Gabriel. And, in a way that he could not explain or begin to understand, Gabriel answered him. He read the angel's responses in his eyes and mouth; these responses were never the same, no matter how often he saw them.

Heller addressed the interloper. 'It's a lovely painting, isn't it?'

'Yes,' Jacob replied, politely.

Heller felt the sweat form on his forehead.

'Did you know that Raphael painted it?' he blurted out, like a child seeking the attention of a preoccupied adult.

The boy nodded his head and looked, for the briefest moment, upon Heller. Shortly afterwards he rose and went on his way. There was no further communication between them.

For days, Heller rehearsed the details of his meeting with the boy in the gallery. He went through what he had said. He dwelt on the memory of the boy's face as he had gazed upon the painting. He remembered his own discomfort. There was something about this boy. Something composed and knowing and unforgiving. And then Heller felt anger mounting in him. Who, he raged to himself, is this boy to hold sway over me?

At home, in the evening, at his writing desk, with Quince upon his lap, Heller brought a new character into the story that he was writing about Rudolfine Prague: a boy called Jan Weiss, the son of a goldsmith. Over his evening meal, he thought about this character. He was, he decided, the son of a foolish man. A man who did occasional work for the emperor, making settings for rare gemstones, rings, amulets and clasps. He pondered how to bring the boy and the emperor together. Then he remembered reading that, as Rudolf's megalomania and paranoia had grown, he had surrounded himself with prattling fools. Emissaries and ambassadors from the great kingdoms of Europe waited for months to be admitted before him, while charlatans were led directly to his quarters. Stable boys enjoyed Rudolf's confidence, while members of the court were snubbed.

So, Heller reasoned, it was possible that in a period of enthusiasm for goldsmithing, Jan's father found himself often in the emperor's presence. Yes, here was a way of bringing the boy and the emperor together. Heller visualised the vain goldsmith, puffed up by the favour he enjoyed with the emperor, referring to his son's gift for predicting the future through prophetic dreams.

'I believe that Jan is inspired by the Divine mind!' the goldsmith boasts. The emperor's attention is awakened.

'Bring the boy,' he says. 'Bring the boy.'

Heller was not sure where his story was heading but he knew that, when he visualised Jan, he saw the boy from the gallery. He wrote:

A groom led the boy into the emperor's apartments and withdrew, pulling the door behind him. Jan felt a momentary flap of panic. He was alone in a cavernous room that was crammed full, like a junk shop. It took him some time before he could distinguish items clearly. A cough startled him. A thin, severe face surveyed him from a writing desk.

'Your Majesty,' Jan stammered, swallowing the knob of saliva that he felt at the back of his throat.

'Lang, Philip Lang, adviser to his majesty.' As Lang uttered the last words, he nodded into the room's interior. The emperor stood smiling at the boy, like someone playing hide-and-seek who had evaded his pursuers.

The emperor was dressed in black in a short tunic and cape, with small stars embroidered on it in gold thread. He wore a white ruff, which emphasised the plumpness of his fleshy face.

'Come, look at this,' he urged Jan, betraying a feverish excitement.

Jan moved to the emperor's side.

'Watch closely, now!' Rudolf moved to a two-foot-high mechanical figure and wound the key in its back. The toy tottered forward on its tin feet.

'Why, sire,' Jan exclaimed, 'it has your likeness.'

'Precisely!' The emperor laughed and the boy shared his pleasure.

'But this is only one of my little men. See, here is a whole army!'

In the hours that followed, Rudolf showed Jan many items in his collection and the boy responded to them with an unfeigned sense of wonder. Jan was not frightened by the emperor. After a while, he was not really conscious of the fact that the man at his side was the emperor. He was more like a toymaster, a child at heart.

Heller laid down his pen.

'Is that how it would be if the boy came here to see my collection?' he wondered aloud. 'He would share my enthusiasm and all barriers would be cast aside?' The idea appealed to him. 'Ah, but would I appear as nothing more than a child, a man afraid to grow up? Is that what a collector is? Yet Rudolf was more than a portly man with a childish enthusiasm for curios and toys; he was the most powerful man of his time. Did Jan see that? He must have. He must have.'

Heller reached for the notebook in which he recorded ideas for his stories. In his copperplate he wrote:

Jan will feel the emperor's wrath and be thrown into the White Tower. And who will save him?

Heller stretched his arms above his head and yawned. It was growing late.

'Who will save my little hero?' he repeated out loud. He considered the familiar figures in Rudolf's story. Rabbi Loew, the Jewish sage who had access to the emperor. The gargantuan Tycho Brahe – he of the metal nose – the aristocratic eccentric who drank himself to death. Or the astronomer Johannes Kepler. He rose from his desk and began moving around his apartment, turning over the possibilities.

'Kepler,' he pronounced out loud. He liked the idea.

Mean, penny-pinching, whining, humourless Kepler, dreamer of dreams. 'He has so little to recommend him as a person, yet how his mind soared above his miserable, wretched little self! Let me make Kepler a hero, Jan's saviour.'

Heller was pleased with himself. His story was taking shape. 'Yes,' he declared, the boy will be saved by the intervention of someone who, for all his failings and pettiness, is a good man.'

*

In the days and weeks that followed, Heller worked on his writing in a feverish, obsessive way. He thought of Jan, the innocent caught in a web of madness and court intrigue. He imagined himself there, as an unseen spectator, and wrote:

Jan had spent many hours in the emperor's company, in the rooms crammed with Rudolf's treasures. Now it was getting late. Still no mention was made of food or leaving. Jan grew uneasy. Rudolf's good spirits had deserted him. The boy waited for an opportunity and then spoke.

'Thank you, Your Majesty, for allowing me to see your wonderful collection. May I come and see it again?'

Rudolf's thick eyebrows rose in a frown, and the ends of his moustache curled upwards.

'Again? What do you mean, again?' he asked, petulantly.

Jan saw the displeasure in Rudolf's face and,

for the first time since meeting him, felt alarmed and afraid of his host.

'It is growing late, sire, and my mother will be anxious for me. I was hoping that you might allow me the honour and privilege of returning to the palace on another day.'

Jan spoke slowly and quietly, trying hard to keep the nervousness from his voice.

'Ah yes, your mother,' Rudolf said absent-mindedly. He pulled on a bell-rope. A groom appeared – out of thin air, it seemed to Jan.

'Send a message to the goldsmith and his wife that the boy will be my guest in the castle for a little time.'

'Yes, Your Majesty,' the groom replied, in a tone and manner that Jan thought insolent.

'A guest, Your Majesty?' he queried, timidly.

'Quite.' There was no disguising the dark cloud that passed over the emperor's face and the sullenness in his puffed cheeks.

Rudolf sat in a large chair. His head sunk on his chest. He said nothing for a little time and, in the silence, Jan heard the beating of his own heart. He feared the anger in the smouldering expression of the man-child, who was his king. He felt he had, somehow, given offence, but was at a loss to understand how or why.

Through the laboured breath of the king, Jan heard the words, 'The dreams. I want your dreams!'

The boy did not know for whom the words were intended. He looked around him. There were others in the room. They materialised like wraiths. Philip Lang, smiling in grim expectation. Strada, the curator of the emperor's collection, tall and thin, with the doleful expression of a cleric. The groom, smirking and superior. All were looking at him, waiting for him to speak.

Jan did not understand what was expected of him. Confusion and ill-defined feelings of guilt rose in him.

'Dreams, Your Majesty?'

'Dreams!' Rudolf screamed, in a fury of impatience that twisted his face into a snarl.

He rose, terrible and cruel, from his seat. 'Give me the future, boy. Do not think to deprive me of it.'

Jan looked to the others for guidance. They stared back at him without responding to the appeal in his face. He turned to the emperor. 'I do not know what you want of me, Your Majesty,' he said in a whisper.

Rudolf stepped back and gripped the chair to steady his trembling body. His breath rose and fell with alarming rapidity. He looked away from Jan as though he found his presence intolerable.

'Give me the future,' he repeated, through clenched teeth.

Jan's head began to spin. He saw his reflection and those of the others in the mirrors facing him. He discerned the shapes of countless items in the emperor's collection in the rooms beyond where he stood. His situation made no sense. He was in the house of the insane, a sleep-walker among dead objects whose shadows danced on the walls in the light of a thousand candles.

Without warning, his legs buckled beneath him and he slumped to the ground. His eyes filled with tears. 'I can't, sire,' was all he could manage. 'Please may I go home?'

Rudolf slumped into his seat, staring into the distance, his face weary and disappointed. He clicked his fingers.

'My cat,' he muttered to the groom. 'Tell them I want my cat.'

'Yes, Your Majesty!' The groom disappeared, Jan sat and cried silent tears, and Rudolf waited for them to bring his pet lion, the only creature on earth who did not disappoint him.

Jan spent the night in the White Tower, the prison that overlooked Stag Moat. The tower stood at the head of Golden Lane, where alchemists were employed to conduct their occult experiments. Rudolf waited eagerly for proof of their success. He needed gold to fuel his growing appetite for rare and precious things, and his fear of death and sickness made him downcast each day. What he wanted from Jan was reassurance. He wanted to be told that death was far off and that wealth beyond all telling was soon to be his. Those who did not give what the emperor wanted languished in the White Tower.

The more Heller thought about his story, the more his obsession with Jacob grew. At lunchtime he made for the gallery, hoping to see the boy. As he walked home from work, he looked at passers-by in the hope of recognising him. A hundred times in the weeks that followed he thought he caught sight of him. Disappearing around a corner. Looking out from the window of a tram. Once he ran after a boy and caught his arm. As the boy turned, Heller noticed the yellow star sewn on the coat. He stood for a moment, lost for words, and the boy took his chance to escape. So, following these failures, he had to content himself with conjuring the boy in his imagination. He continued with his writing:

A jailer roused Jan from his misery and marched him along the stone corridors that led back to the living quarters. Jan had not suspected that fear is a physical phenomenon, something that lodges in your gut and will not be moved. He had not imagined that fear is a weight you struggle to carry in your aching arms. He had not realised that fear plays tricks with your eyes so that you stumble over obstacles that you cannot see. Fear invaded every fibre of Jan's being. He was desperate to escape its embrace. Yet it suffocated him and did not allow him to think clearly.

Trembling and snivelling, he was led before the emperor. This time Rudolf sat on his throne in a great hall illuminated by a thousand candles. There were others attending him. Two stood near the throne. There was a gargantuan man, with a head bald as an egg and a moustache that twisted and curled beyond his cheeks. This was Tycho Brahe, the court astronomer. Beside him was a little man of sickly complexion with an avid look and clothes that were formal but used and stained. This was Johannes Kepler. Rudolf wanted their opinion of the boy.

Jan fell at the emperor's feet and, without waiting for a command, blurted out, 'Your majesty, I have dreamed during the night.'

Fear gripped him tighter and the words were forced from his mouth. They tumbled out in a rush of air. 'There were dolphins riding the seas and whales and all manner of great fish. And the sun, Your Majesty, yes, the sun shone on the sea and made a rainbow and the sky was filled with birds.'

Jan was now kneeling upright, driven there by terror. His voice grew stronger and the words clearer. 'There was a lion flying in the sky above the rainbow. In the distant sky I saw the royal palace, Your Majesty.'

Jan paused and Rudolf leaned forward. 'A flying lion? Are you sure?

'Yes, Your Majesty.'

'But what does it mean?'

Jan felt the weight of despair begin to crush him. With tears smarting in his eyes he whispered, 'I do not know, Your Majesty.' He bowed his head and waited for the sentence of the emperor. But it was not the voice of Rudolf that sounded in his ear.

'Allow me, Your Majesty, to take the boy and record this and other of his dreams. I will consider them and examine the stars and cast your horoscope. There are mysteries here that bespeak the gift of vision.'

The emperor turned with an eager, hopeful expression to the speaker. 'Continue,' he commanded.

'The fish and the ocean are the world of hidden knowledge and wonder, which you, above all living men, appreciate. The flying lion is the symbol of the evangelist Mark, keeper of the Word. The rainbow speaks of God's favour. The castle tells us that you are the favoured one.'

Rudolf's hand went to his beard and stroked it. 'Indeed. Then you believe, Kepler, that the boy can see into the heart of things?'

'I believe, Your Majesty, there is a gift in the boy's seeing.'

Jan knelt upright, watching in wonder the face of the man who was his champion. The other one, the gargantuan, coughed, as if to check his companion's foolishness. But the thin one stepped forward, closer to the emperor.

'Allow me to add my skill to the boy's gift and we will see if the heavenly bodies agree with the boy's dreams,' he said.

'Two days.' Rudolf rose from the throne and, pulling his cloak around his dumpy body, made his way into the labyrinth that was his home and his prison. There was animated talk and some mocking laughter, directed at Kepler, after the emperor withdrew. The little man ignored it.

'Come,' Kepler said to Jan, without any trace of warmth.

Jan did as he was told. As the boy followed his saviour, Brahe spoke. 'What streak of self-destruction is there in you, Kepler, that you cannot keep your tongue in your pox-scarred head when you should. And yet I've seen you fall as silent as a timid maid when I needed you to speak. This foolishness, this nonsense will bring ruin upon your head. Do not expect me, Tycho Brahe, to deliver you from the calamity that will befall you. And all this for a whingeing child!' Brahe concluded his speech by spitting phlegm on the stone floor of the castle.

Heller sat in his armchair sipping a glass of wine. Of course, there was no evidence that Kepler was the kind-hearted man of his story. But it was not beyond the bounds of possibility that he would take pity on the plight of a young boy, the victim of a father's foolishness and an emperor's madness. After all, Kepler's own father was a vicious wastrel. Kepler knew the misfortune of having a foolish parent and had suffered in his childhood. He had been the victim of constant illness and poor health and was scarred from innumerable boils and infected sores, so that he hated his own body and thought of himself as no better than a mangy dog. Such a man might be moved to pity a boy's terror. In rescuing Jan, Kepler was seeking to rescue himself.

*

Heller was sitting on his seat before the *Madonna* on a Saturday afternoon when Jacob came and sat alongside him. As before, the boy gave all his attention to the painting. Heller felt a wave of envy wash over him. Suddenly, it mattered to him to break the boy's concentration. He wanted to assert his power over this child, to master him. He addressed Jacob.

'Hello, do you remember me from the last time we met?'

'Hello. Yes, I remember you.'

'Good.'

There was a brief silence. When Heller spoke again there was an edge to his voice. 'That painting could not have been done by a modern painter. The work of modern painters glorifies what is ugly. Don't you agree?'

Heller's outburst was greeted by a nervous cough from the boy.

'Mark my words,' Heller resumed, 'modern painters are the corrupters of the human mind. They seek to spread filth and ugliness and call it art. But they would not succeed were it not for the filthy Jews who support them. Artists? How dare they call themselves artists! They are . . .' Heller paused, losing his train of thought, but at least, he noted with grim satisfaction, he had the boy's attention.

Jacob was upset by the stranger's onslaught. He thought of his father and mother and their love of art. Were they 'filthy Jews'? Hardly. He wanted to protest but this man frightened him. He felt trapped.

Heller, for his part, fell silent. The sound of his voice, shrill and irrational, echoed in his mind. He was embarrassed. He wanted the boy to smile so that he could excuse his ridiculous outburst. But Jacob hung his head, mumbling that his mother was waiting. And then he stood and bolted for home.

For days, Jacob moped about, oppressed and defeated, reliving the encounter in the gallery. He hated himself for his lack of courage, his failure of nerve, his silence.

10

A MURDER AT COURT

Urbino, Autumn 1511

The festivities lasted a week. On the second day after the wedding, the Pope and his entourage left in a blaze of dust that could be seen for miles. Francesco and Castiglione professed themselves well pleased with the outcome of the Papal visit. On the same day, Elizabeth and the Gonzaga family left for Mantua. Andrea contrived to position himself in Elizabeth's line of vision as the carriage set off. She met his eye and waved cheerfully to him.

Other guests lingered to make the most of the occasion – to feed and drink at the duke's expense. Among them was Cardinal Giulio Chesi, a member of a wealthy Florentine family with close links to the powerful Medicis. Andrea noticed how Francesco acted with great cordiality towards this important guest and, though the youth had seen enough of court life to mistrust appearances, he could not have suspected the duke's hatred of this man or guessed at his murderous intentions. Chesi was suspected by Francesco of being one of those who had betrayed him to the Bolognese, though Francesco had never given any hint of his suspicion. On the contrary, he had worked to win the trust of the cardinal. But all the while, he had been biding his time and plotting his revenge. Now, restored to favour with Rome, Francesco decided to act.

After the departure of Elizabeth, Andrea fell into a state of despondency. It suited his mood to find that Castiglione was irritable and impatient with the fact that so many people remained in the palace. It suited his mood that Castiglione summoned him to help with the filing and cataloguing of a mountain of papers and books. The two worked side by side, saying little to each other. They were interrupted by the arrival of the captain of the guard who approached and whispered urgently into Castiglione's ear. The courtier immediately rose from his work.

'Come, boy,' he called to Andrea, ' you might as well see for yourself the workings of the court.'

Andrea was perplexed by the tone of this invitation. It spoke of loathing, disgust and triumph all at once. He felt the air of suppressed excitement as he followed the two men down passages and stairways. Then, before he knew it, he was standing in a bedroom. Andrea felt nervous, fearing what he might see. But the room was empty. Then they were in a narrow passageway, which, somehow, led to another room. And there on the floor lay the body of Cardinal Giulio Chesi, his head resting on his twisted right arm. The prelate's nightgown was caught above the knees, exposing the pale skin of his slender legs. In the light, Andrea could see the legs' soft, downy hair and he felt embarrassed at seeing a human being so open to scrutiny and inspection, even as his eyes took in the details of the scene.

Castiglione showed no interest in the corpse. Instead he searched for the cardinal's private journal and handed it to his page. Then he substituted the tumbler in the room for one he had brought with him. He moved quickly but without panic or flurry. He ordered Andrea to open the shutters and leave them ajar. He inspected the room and pronounced himself satisfied, nodding his approval to the captain, who led them back the way they had come.

Andrea's head was a whirl of ideas, speculation and half-understandings. He was not disturbed by the fact of a death. He had twisted the necks of chickens and helped his father slit the throat of a pig. And five children – one of them Andrea's twin – borne by his mother had died in infancy. But he had never encountered death in this guise before – death planned and plotted – and it filled him with a vague sensation of distaste and dread. This distaste sharpened and directed itself towards the retreating figure of Castiglione and the ease with which the elegant courtier had involved himself in this murder.

Castiglione went directly to Francesco's apartments, bidding Andrea wait in the anteroom, the same room he had stood in with his father. But now Andrea had little thought of the fireplaces or the leaping dolphins. He leant against the door and heard the voice of the duke.

'You bring news of the poxed prelate?' Francesco asked.

Andrea could not catch Castiglione's words but he heard the duke's laughter. 'You are a ministering angel, Baldassare.'

Andrea caught snatches of the conversation. The duke was satisfied that Rome would be pleased by the death of Chesi and was confident that the investigating magistrate could be persuaded to lay the blame for it far from his door.

Having gleaned as much as he could, Andrea retreated to the far end of the room to wait for his master. Presently,

Castiglione appeared and ordered him to summon the captain of the guard to the duke. Some time later, a small group assembled in the duke's private apartment. Among them were the magistrate and his notary, who made a record of all that was said. Andrea had acquired the page's knack of making himself almost invisible. He knew that as long as he was quiet and still Castiglione would permit him to remain.

The civic magistrate was required to investigate the murder. As the victim was a cardinal, a report would have to be sent to the Vatican. Andrea recognised that the magistrate was ill at ease in the company of the duke. Francesco, for his part, sat half turned away from the officials, feigning an air of irritation at the proceedings. It was Castiglione who controlled the unfolding drama.

'Your honour,' he began, addressing the magistrate, 'I believe the captain has looked into the matter. Perhaps you would like to hear his findings?'

'Ah, yes, thank you, Signor Castiglione. Captain?'

The captain spoke clearly and to the point. 'Since discovering the body of the prelate, I have made enquiries of my men. I have learnt that on the day of the wedding the sentries on duty saw the Cevas brothers in the crowd. They took no action, as they believed that the brothers had come, like everyone else, to join in the celebrations. There was nothing in their behaviour to suggest that they were planning anything underhand. In fact they made no effort to hide their presence or to disguise themselves'

Here the captain paused and Castiglione spoke. 'What, you may ask, your honour, is the importance of this report?'

'Indeed,' replied the magistrate, 'the question was on the tip of my tongue.'

'These brothers were sworn enemies of the dead

prelate,' Castiglione continued. 'The sentries, of course, were not to know this. But before many members of the court, myself included, the cardinal had spoken of the ill will these men bore him. It played on his mind. I need hardly remind your honour of the crimes these men are reputed to have committed. Only now do we see the murderous nature of the hatred the Cevas bore our esteemed and lamented friend.'

Castiglione paused for his revelation to have its full effect. He apologised for having interrupted the proceedings and invited the captain to resume giving his evidence.

'The cause of the cardinal's death was poison,' the captain said. A tumbler, found in the chamber, had traces of poisonous substance on the rim.'

At this point, Andrea allowed himself to steal a glance at Castiglione. His master stood impassively.

'There was no evidence,' continued the captain, 'of a forced entry into the room, but the chambermaid, who last evening left a jug of water and a glass there for the prelate's use, did recall leaving the shutters open to allow the air to circulate. It is my belief, your honour, that the Cevas brothers stole into the palace and climbed to the open window of the prelate's chamber. They entered the room, poisoned the water and made good their escape through the same window. The unsuspecting prelate returned to his room, drank the water and after a little time fell dead. We are not sure how these notorious criminals knew the room. We can only guess that they may have had a spy within the household staff. I have arranged to interview all the palace servants to find out who the spy is. Either that or the brothers were in league with a member of the visiting delegations.'

Here the captain drew breath, pleased with his work. The magistrate thanked him.

'Who, good captain, discovered the body?' he asked.

There was a momentary flap of panic on the captain's part. Castiglione had not anticipated this question and had not rehearsed with the captain how he should answer it.

'The . . . maid. The maid. She then alerted the sentries, who, in turn, alerted me, and I informed Signor Castiglione, who summoned the physician.'

'So,' resumed the magistrate, 'the prelate had not left his key in the lock, given that the maid could gain admittance to the room? And if she gained admittance, someone else with a key might also have done so?'

The captain looked to Castiglione for help. Even the notary raised his head to observe the two men.

'But surely that is of no consequence?' suggested Castiglione.

'Well, perhaps not,' the magistrate replied, holding Castiglione's gaze until the courtier dropped his eyes.

During this time, the duke had retained his pose of studied indifference. Now he faced the magistrate and rose to his feet.

'The case is clear, your honour, is it not? The Cevas brothers have gained entry to my palace, through a window or through a door – that hardly matters – and have poisoned my guest. It is an outrage against the Pope and against me. God will it that I avenge this death upon them. My captain and Signor Castiglione are at your disposal. Make your report and send it to the Vatican with all possible haste.'

The duke began to move towards the door. 'And be sure that I get a copy of it before it is sent. Do you understand?' There was no disguising the menace in the duke's final remarks.

'Your wish is my command, Your Excellency.'

'Good. And now, gentlemen, forgive me, I am tired and will to bed.'

With that the duke left the room and Castiglione invited the magistrate to view the scene of the crime.

11

A SECOND CHANCE

Dresden, 1995

When Jacob and his grandson, Ben, come to stand before
Raphael's masterpiece, *The Sistine Madonna*, in the Gallery
of Old Masters in Dresden, Jacob feels none of the
emotions he has anticipated. Inwardly, he has steeled
himself against the pain of remembering his mother. But
there is no pain on that account. Instead, his memory is
invaded by a scene he has not brought to mind for many
years – decades, even. He is sitting side by side with Franz
Heller in front of this very painting. People are passing
to and fro within feet of them but he and Heller are
isolated, removed from the passers-by. Eyes closed, fists
clenched, Jacob tries to ward off the words of the menacing
stranger. But try as he might, his whole being is compressed into hearing, and the word 'corruption' occupies
every space in his brain till he fears that his head will
burst. And then he is on his feet and fleeing through the
labyrinth of rooms and corridors.

Jacob's recall of the scene is vivid and complete. It
startles but does not upset him. He touches Ben's
shoulder.

'You go ahead,' he whispers. 'I'm going to sit over

there for a while.'

'Are you all right, Grandad?'

'Don't fuss, Benjamin.'

'There's no need to bite my head off.'

'Go on, off you go,' says Jacob, without smiling.

'Well, see you later then,' says Ben, as he moves away, not quite sure what he should do.

Jacob sits. He knows there are memories to be inspected. He waits. He is curious, like a tourist revisiting a city after many years' absence. Curious and mildly excited and fearful of disappointment. And then, like a tourist, he finds himself where he does not expect to be.

He is in a dream. He is running down a long gallery. On either side there are large, imposing portraits. Eighteenth-century portraits of men with big heads, bulbous noses and protruding eyes mouthing the word 'corruption'. Every face twisted and grimacing. There is no escape. The sides are closing in, and behind him, clear and distinct, he hears footsteps. Heller's footsteps, no doubt. No choice but to keep running. But the more he hurries, the more the gallery stretches into the distance. And then his legs refuse to obey him. They will not go forward. The sides are squashing in on him, the footsteps louder, and his legs refuse to budge. He looks down and sees that a serpent has coiled itself round his limbs. He screams aloud and the echo mocks him.

Sitting quiet and dignified in his dark suit and wine-coloured bow tie, Jacob, his black hair and beard flecked silvery-grey, might pass for a professor of art history. He sits back, with his hands crossed on the cane planted between his feet. He has forgotten the measure of his terror, the unsettling disturbance Heller caused in him. And he has forgotten – or may never have realised until this moment – the misery of his tormentor.

Jacob's mind turns over the mystery of meeting Heller in this gallery before this painting so many years ago. Could the crossing of their paths have been foreseen? Is it possible to know, from where you start, where you will arrive? No, he concludes, all is chance and uncertainty. Take this painting, this inheritance from another world – this too is chance. Out of the hustle and bustle, the greed and envy of his world, Raphael snatched the stillness of the *Madonna*. As in every century, painters make their marks and create still moments. Wassily Kandinsky, for example, a friend of his father. Why had he not laughed at Heller's talk of corruption, or explained patiently to him, as to a child? And Jacob begins to speak softly to the ghost of Franz Heller sitting beside him.

'Do you think, Herr Heller, that there is a shade of blue to fit every emotion? I do. For me, blue is not the colour of sadness; it is the colour of infinite possibility – the blue of the Mediterranean, the blue of Tiepolo, the blue of this Madonna's gown. Wassily Kandinsky gave our family a gift, a painting of a village – I think it was called Murnau – which was very beautiful and filled with blue – clouds and fields and towers of blue. No, Herr Heller, you are wrong to think the modern imagination is sordid. Life is sordid. The death camps are sordid. But you cannot blame the painters for that.'

Jacob stops. The sixty-five-year-old tourist, who looks like a professor, feels good. He has found the words that were needed. But there is something more to his satis-faction. In revisiting this scene, he experiences a remark-able sensation. As he speaks he knows that he is speaking as his father would have spoken. He knows that he has stumbled, somehow, into his father's mind. And, through his father's eyes, he sees the crumpled, middle-aged figure of the lonely Franz Heller. And Jacob feels pity for him.

Ben comes back. 'Are you OK?'

'Fine, thank you, though I'd like some coffee.'

'But we've travelled so far, Grandad, and you've hardly looked at anything,' Ben protests.

'Don't prattle, Benjamin. You sound like your mother,' Jacob remarks drily, and Ben, fearing one of Jacob's dark moods, falls silent. But his fears are groundless, for Jacob is well satisfied with his morning's work and he tells his grandson a little of Franz Heller.

'When I was your age, or thereabouts, I met a man here who played a large part in my life. I think, perhaps, that I owe my life to him.'

'I thought you owed your life to an angel, Grandad.'

Jacob laughs. 'Maybe Franz Heller was an angel. Though I did not think so when I first met him. One day he sat beside me in this very gallery and spoke wild, senseless things about art and artists. I was so frightened that I ran all the way home.'

'And what happened?'

'Well, I stopped coming to the gallery. But by chance, when I was out walking with Mother, he approached us and apologised for his behaviour. She didn't know what he was talking about because I hadn't said a word to her about what had happened. And then Heller, on a sudden impulse – at least I think it was a sudden impulse – invited us to dine with him at his apartment. And mother, who was normally so cautious and wary of people, accepted the invitation without hesitation.'

'And did you go?'

'Yes.'

'And?'

'And Heller became a kind of friend to us.'

'Is that all?'

Jacob laughs. 'I'm sorry to disappoint you, Ben, but that is all.'

Ben appraises his grandfather. 'I don't think you're telling me everything,' he says in a playful, impudent way. 'Was there something between them?'

'No, not that kind of something.'

'Do you think you could find Heller's apartment?' Ben asks with sudden enthusiasm.

'I'm not sure I want to find it. Anyway, why would you like to find it?'

'To have a memory of it.'

Jacob smiles. 'We'll see,' he concedes, in response to the boy's cunning.

12

VAGABONDS

Rome, Spring 1512

The investigating magistrate made his report on the murder of Cardinal Giulio Chesi and named the Cevas brothers as the chief suspects. Within a few short weeks the matter was forgotten by all but a small number of people at court. But Andrea could not rid his mind of the sight of the dead man and his pale, sickly legs, and though Castiglione was as charming as ever, his page now looked on him with fascinated revulsion. So, with the permission of his master, Andrea spent most of his time with Timoteo Viti, painting as he had never done before. Painting to escape; painting to forget.

Timoteo Viti was working on a commission for a convent just outside Urbino. He was renowned for his interpretation of the stories of the Old Testament. The stories of Moses and Noah and the other Patriarchs came to life in his hands. This work was to show Jacob receiving the blessing of his father, Isaac. Viti was enthused by the subject.

'Did you know, Andrea, that "Jacob" is the Hebrew for "heel"?'

'No.'

'Let me tell you the story.'

Andrea nodded, more out of politeness than interest. But Timoteo was warming to his theme.

'Jacob was a twin. His brother was Esau and his parents were Isaac and Rebekah. Esau was bigger and stronger than Jacob. He was also the first-born.' Here the painter stopped, standing back from the panel to inspect the progress he had made. He was tracing the design onto the surface of the wood. Normally Andrea would have worked with his master, but today he sketched and painted his own works, and Viti left him alone, sensing that the youth was distracted. Satisfied, the painter continued.

'When Esau emerged from his mother's womb, his little brother, Jacob, was clinging to his heel. You see, even in the womb, the little one was a fighter. And that is how he got his name.' Viti paused, waiting for the response that he felt the story deserved. But none came. So he resumed his tale, pondering Andrea's mood and watching him without pretending to do so.

'As they grew, Esau was their father's favourite. A great, red, hairy fellow he was – an outdoor boy. He loved to hunt, fish and fight. Not so his little brother, who was doted on by their mother. When the time came for Isaac to give his blessing to his first-born, Rebekah helped Jacob to deceive his father. It wasn't too hard a task, for Isaac was an old man and his sight was weak. Even so, Jacob was cunning. He dressed himself in goat hide so that, when his father laid hands upon him, he felt the rough, hairy skin and believed it to be that of his beloved Esau. Then Isaac blessed the boy and called upon God to make him prosper.'

Andrea had not really listened to Timoteo's tale, yet it

entered his mind and stayed there. He had never given much thought to his twin who had died at birth. This brother was a shadowy figure, vague and distant. But the murder of Cardinal Chesi and the story of Esau and Jacob brought frightening ideas to Andrea. Then he began to dream, and the same dream haunted his sleep for nights.

In the dream Andrea is swimming under water. Above him there is light, but it is far away and faint. He knows that he must reach the light. He faces upwards and kicks with all his might. But he is held down. There is something impeding him. He looks down into the murky water. Jacob, his twin, clings to his heel. His brother is struggling to keep up with him. This angers Andrea. He looks to the light. It is so far away. His lungs are bursting. He must get to the surface. Gathering his strength, he kicks with all his might. But Jacob will not be shaken off. Desperate, Andrea looks to the light. It hits the water and diffuses into a rainbow.

Andrea decides now what he must do. He doubles back. Jacob's birth cord dangles from his navel. Andrea seizes the cord and wraps it around his brother's neck. He pulls it tight. Jacob releases his hold of Andrea and struggles to loosen the cord. As his brother fights for his breath, Andrea holds his arms above his head and kicks upwards. The light grows stronger. Andrea's head breaks the surface. He is surrounded by light. He opens his mouth and gulps in the air. He is born, warm in the sun beyond the waters.

Now the dream changes. There is a fishing boat. The fishermen prepare to gather in their catch. They pull on the ropes. There is a child in the net. His umbilical cord is wrapped around his neck. Dressed in a goatskin, Jacob looks down upon his dead brother, caught in the net of the fishermen. There is sudden laughter. Francesco della

Rovere and Baldassare Castiglione are beside him, clapping him on the back, congratulating him.

Each night at this point in the dream, Andrea woke proclaiming his innocence, beset by fear and guilt. He knew that he had to escape Urbino to end his nightmares.

Andrea opened his heart, insofar as he dared, to Timoteo Viti. Andrea said enough to convince him that he needed to get away from Urbino. Thus it was that Viti wrote to Raphael asking whether the offer of an apprenticeship was still open.

For a time nothing was heard from Rome, and then in the early spring of 1512 a note, short and to the point, came from Raphael, stating that Andrea was welcome to join his studio. Francesco cared little whether Andrea stayed or left. Castiglione was saddened by the news, though he did not stand in Andrea's way and guessed at the reasons for his departure. And so it came to pass that Andrea, fearful of what lay ahead yet troubled by what he knew, left Urbino and Timoteo Viti and travelled to Rome to begin a new life in the workshop of Raphael Santi.

Andrea travelled with a convoy of merchants. He wore the livery of the della Rovere family and carried a letter of greeting from the duke and commendations from Castiglione and Viti. In his purse was more money than he had ever possessed in his life. Before setting out, Andrea had written hastily to Menocchio, and, though he had written, 'Word has come from Rome from Raphael for me to join his workshop', he did not really believe it was true. But here he was, sleeping at an inn, a day's journey from the great city and the great man who was to be his master.

As he neared his journey's end, fear and doubt beset

him and gripped his heart. For all his letters of introduction and fine clothes, Andrea was young and naive and knew himself to be so. The rough manner of the merchants, their worldly talk of commerce and profit and their jokes about their wives and mistresses made him uncomfortable. They laughed and jeered at him and he did not know how to respond. So he recalled the image of Raphael greeting Pope Julius in Urbino. He remembered the easy charm of the painter, his mild manner, his graciousness. But the memory was little proof against the dirty blankets of the inn and its thin walls, through which the sounds of carousing and dark laughter invaded his room.

The convoy arrived in Rome in the early afternoon. Andrea alighted from the cart on which he had travelled and took leave of his companions. He had no clear plan. He simply took off in the direction in which he was facing, carrying his bundle of clothes and a packet containing his painting materials. The city was dazzling: big, noisy, smelly, chaotic and with more people than he had thought it possible for a city to contain. Splendour and filth existed side by side. It seemed that he proceeded by spinning, so often did he find himself turning this way and that to follow the path of someone who caught his eye or to take in a building or a ruin.

The artist in him wanted to stand still, take paper and pen and catch all he saw. Near the Coliseum, he plucked up the courage to sit at a table at an inn. He sketched quickly, tracing the curving lines of the great building against a backdrop of trees – the ubiquitous umbrella pine of the city and some mighty oaks, under whose shade the weary rested. Then he was up and wandering again, finding the Tiber and following its course till he found St Peter's Piazza.

The square was thronged with pilgrims, priests, tradesmen and stallholders. There was a great deal of activity around the basilica. The foundations for the new church could be seen, and parts of the old one had already been demolished. Andrea made his way through the crowds and entered St Peter's. There was much to see – too much – but he had determined to limit himself to surveying one work of art. It was placed in a small chapel off the nave, near the main entrance. Andrea was fortunate. There were only a few others there. They were not Italian – Flemish perhaps – and they chatted amiably and pointed to this and that before moving off, leaving the chapel to Andrea.

Never before had he seen such beauty in a piece of sculpture. His trained eye observed that the body of the prone Christ was disproportionately small and the Virgin's lap too wide. But the more he looked, the more he lost himself in the smooth, polished marble and in the wondrous folds of the Virgin's garments. Timoteo Viti had urged him to study Michelangelo's *Pieta*. How right his former master had been.

Andrea left the basilica in a rush. To the west he could see trees and blue sky. He made for them, leaving the city behind. He wanted time to dwell on the beauty of what he had seen. He wanted solitude. He found a glade in an area of light woodland and stretched himself on the ground. He lay there, recalling every detail of the sculpture. Overcome by delight and nervous exhaustion, he closed his eyes and fell into a deep sleep. He dreamed of angels bearing aloft the prone body of the crucified Christ while angelic hosts sang hosannas, and then he dreamed of dark passageways and a cardinal writhing in his death throes. Then it was Andrea himself who lay prone on a great plain while a fiery angel swept low over the earth with his terrible, gleaming sword.

When Andrea woke, the sun had gone from the sky and he was cold and stiff. He searched his bundle and found his woollen cloak. He was hungry and, though it was near to nightfall, he had made no attempt to find Raphael's residence or workshop. He had the address, but there was a deep reluctance within him, born of self-doubt and fear. What if his reception was as unwelcoming as the one he had received from Francesco della Rovere when he had travelled to Urbino with his father? In his time at court he had become a favourite with the courtiers. What would Raphael's assistants make of him? Would they laugh at his manners and way of talking? Was his talent great enough? All these misgivings sat heavy upon him, so he was almost pleased that it was dark and the inevitable could be postponed a little longer.

But there was the immediate matter of finding a place to stay and some food. He stood upright and surveyed the surrounding countryside. There were no lights visible, but he did see smoke rising in the woods not too far from where he was and, without giving a great deal of thought to the wisdom of what he was doing, he made for the woods.

The smoke came from the fire of a ragged troupe of travelling players and entertainers who were making camp for the night. As Andrea approached, two half-starved dogs came bounding towards him, growling and showing their evil-looking teeth. A man rose from his place at the fire and looked to see what the commotion was. When he saw the boy, he laughed.

'A lad come to audition for our distinguished troupe,' he said. And, picking up a handful of dirt, he threw it at the hounds. 'Go to blazes, you lice-infected sacks of bone!' he shouted at them.

The dogs yelped and slunk away under a cart. Now the small group was on its feet and standing in a semicircle, gazing in disbelief at the youthful courtier who had walked out of the forest into their camp.

'Jesu Maria! Where has this dressed-up mannequin come from?' a dark-haired woman asked, her eyes wide and smiling. 'Don't stand there like a half-wit, come in and warm yourself.'

There were six in the group: two youths who were little more than his own age, the woman who had spoken and three men. The leader was a heavy-set man who wore a sheepskin jerkin. His hair and beard were long and fine, like a youth's. He had a broad forehead and pale eyes, and his gaze was shrewd and penetrating.

'Do not look so startled, young fellow,' he said. 'True, we are hungry, but we have not yet sunk to eating lost souls.'

Another man, who was huddled in a threadbare cloak and had reseated himself close to the fire, muttered, 'Not yet!' One of the youths laughed and turned a cartwheel and then bowed to the young courtier.

'At your service, young gentleman. There is no duty I will not perform for you, if the price is right.' Andrea bowed, unsure of his ground among the mocking destitution of the troupe.

'Keep clear of that whoreson, young fellow,' the one wrapped in the cloak growled.

'Shame on you, you besmirch my reputation,' the youth retorted, smiling all the while at Andrea and showing his yellow teeth.

'Aye, and for the right price I'd cut your throat,' said the other youth, dressed in the particoloured costume of a clown. So saying, he took a broad-bladed knife from his belt and, with speed and precision, threw it at a tree. He too turned and bowed to the new arrival.

The woman advanced and put a protective arm around Andrea.

'Leave our guest alone. Have you been walking far?' she enquired, solicitously, guiding him towards the fire and handing his bundle and package to an old man. This man, who was wearing a fustian gown like that of a monk, received the items and moved off beyond the circle of light.

'No, I arrived in Rome today from Urbino. I am a painter and am to join the workshop of Raphael Santi,' said Andrea with self-conscious pride.

'And your livery?' the leader asked, touching Andrea's new doublet with the end of the stick he carried. Andrea was not deaf to the mixture of envy and contempt in the question.

'The della Rovere family. I was in the employ of the Duke of Urbino, nephew of the Pope.'

The last part of the statement was uttered with growing confidence. Andrea, after all, knew the power of Francesco and Julius.

'"The employ of the duke",' the first youth said, mimicking Andrea and lisping his words to gain a comical effect. There was laughter. The youth grew bold. He advanced towards the seated Andrea and stood over him.

'The Pope's rule does not extend into the forest at night, young gentleman. Neither your fine clothes,' and here he gripped Andrea's doublet and pulled him closer to him, 'nor your mincing speech will afford you much protection.'

Andrea felt the blood rise to his cheeks. He was not accustomed to rough treatment and he was afraid. But he was also angry: he had done or said nothing to harm this youth. Fear and anger combined to give him a surge of strength and daring. He moved his body forward, closer to his adversary and, grabbing hold of the other's jerkin, threw himself back with all his force. The youth fell forward and Andrea, rolling quickly, had him stretched on the ground and pinioned with his knees and hands. As he rolled, he snatched a handful of dirt and stuffed it into the mouth of the youth who, coughing and spluttering, begged for mercy. The leader, laughing heartily, put a restraining hand on Andrea's shoulder and bid him be at peace.

'Bravo, my little courtier,' he cried. And, shaking his finger at the prone member of his troupe, he warned, 'Your mouth, Sebastian, is the bravest part of you. You fight like a shrew! And how many times have I told you not to judge a book by its cover?'

The youth turned his head and spat out the dirt. Andrea carefully released his hold but his opponent made no attempt to rise.

Once again the woman was at Andrea's side. She led him to the fire.

'Be calm, now, my desperado,' she said, in a tone that was at once soothing and gibing. 'Father Time,' she called to the old man, 'bring some wine and bread for our victor,' and she put one end of her shawl around Andrea's shoulder and the other round her own.

The food and drink arrived and Andrea ate and drank with a ravenous appetite. The woman played him like a guitar, drawing out all his history, including his love for Elizabeth and his knowledge concerning the murder of

Cardinal Chesi, but, drunk as he was from the strong wine, he did not reveal the part Castiglione and the duke had played in the affair. And, as night drew in, the woman spoke endearments in his ear and placed little kisses on his head, and Andrea called her Elizabeth and kissed her dark ringlets.

In the morning, when he woke, with his head aching and every movement causing it to throb violently, Andrea brought to mind the knotted hair and the thin, pinched face of the woman. He remembered her sweaty smell and, thus remembering, his stomach heaved and he fell to his knees and was sick.

When he rose, he saw the wine stains and dirt on his fine clothes. He looked around. The embers of the fire glowed faintly but the troupe had struck camp. He sat on the ground and felt for his boots. They were not to be found. Neither was his bundle of clothes nor his artist's materials. Now Andrea was on his hands and knees frantically searching for his possessions, knowing that it was useless to look for them. As he scratched here and there, he put his hand to his belt and discovered that his purse was gone too.

He stopped his futile searching and sat back on his hunkers. He looked up. The sky was clear and blue but he could not bear to look upon it. He lowered his head and put his hands over his face. His boots, clothes, material and money were all gone. And he remembered vaguely his talk to the woman by the campfire. Loose talk of the kind he prided himself on never speaking. But there was worse to come. Slowly he opened his eyes and held his hands before them. His ring, the one that Elizabeth had given him, was gone.

Andrea Doni had arrived in Rome.

13

REVELATIONS

Dresden, Summer 1944

It was the first time since he had come to Dresden that Franz Heller had entertained anyone in his apartment. Except for the cleaning lady, no one had seen his precious collection. As the time approached for the arrival of his guests, Heller felt nervous and checked his appearance in the mirror. He adjusted his tiepin, pulled his waistcoat down and straightened his cuffs. Stepping back, he surveyed himself from head to toe, twisting this way and that. When he had completed the inspection, he allowed himself a smile. True, his hair was greying, but his figure was trim and compact.

'What do you think, Quince,' he demanded of his cat. 'Not too bad, eh?'

He now turned his attention to the dinner table. He had purchased a white damask cloth for the occasion. The cutlery had a high sheen. The linen napkins were starched and the crystal caught the light of the candles.

'Yes,' Heller said aloud, 'very good.'

He rubbed his hands in anticipation, like a little boy. He had not felt such a lightness of spirit for years.

And then his guests arrived. When the greetings and

welcomes were over, Heller called on Maria and Jacob to look over his treasures. He showed them various shells and recited a litany of names: Martin's Tibia, Pagoda, Spiral Babylon, Butterfly Cone, Chorus Mussel, Little Bear Conch, Wandering Triton. Like the rare words that he noted and sought to use in his writing, these names formed part of his possessions.

'Come, look at these,' he urged, gesturing towards the shelves that held the stones and minerals. Jacob hung back, distrustful of the fervour Heller brought to his hobby. The boy did not want to handle the pieces in the collection.

Heller noted – and misunderstood – Jacob's reluctance. 'Do not fear, Jacob, there is no danger of damaging anything and, besides, there is nothing of value to break.' Heller laughed. 'My stones are precious because I have ordained it so. Among my children I am god.'

He aimed a smile at Jacob, who responded in a half-hearted way, for he found Heller's talk odd and unnerving. Nor had he forgotten the haranguing he had received in the gallery. Then his host handed him a shell. It was white and translucent.

'Hold it to the light,' Heller suggested.

Jacob held it aloft. The effect was beautiful: delicate and changing.

'Ah, see now, young man, you are falling under their spell. Look, look at this.' And he held up a high-spired shell with an elongated tail. 'This is the umbilicus.'

Jacob replaced his shell and moved off. He picked up a gemstone. 'Please tell me about this one, Herr Heller.'

'That is one of my favourites. It is amethyst. Do you know that its name means "not intoxicated"?'

'No, I didn't,' Maria replied, charmed by the boyish quality in Heller's excitement. And so the evening got under way.

Then they sat down to eat. Heller brought plates and dishes, which were covered with linen cloths, to the table. Food was scarce in Dresden. For the last year or so, the inhabitants had eaten little more than potatoes and cabbage. Meat was difficult to get; most of it had been requisitioned for the army. So, with no little pride and a theatrical flourish, Heller removed the coverings and invited his guests to help themselves. He had done well. There were salads, breads and pastas. But the main platters contained sausage meat of various kinds. Jacob blanched. As a family, they had always eaten kosher food. Jacob's grandfather had been a strict observer of Jewish law. Benjamin, Jacob's father, did not share his father's views, but he had never acquired a liking for pork. And Jacob, in his thirteen years, had never tasted it. And here were platters with pork meat in abundance.

Heller was the perfect host, attentive to his guests' every need. He noticed the little portions of meat that Jacob took. Mistaking his reluctance for shyness, he heaped the boy's plate, joking about a growing lad and his need for nourishment.

Jacob tried his best to hide his qualms. He joined in the conversation and ate the food as nonchalantly as he could, trying not to taste the offending meat as he chewed it. But it was to no avail. There was no countering the feeling of nausea that beset him. Hurriedly he lay down his knife and fork and excused himself from the table. From the bathroom they heard him retching. Maria looked at Heller's face. She saw in his eyes that he understood what was happening.

'Excuse me, Herr Heller, I must go to him.'

Her host rose and waited for her to leave the table.

Maria emerged a little time later.

'He is weak and overcome. It would assist him greatly if he could lie down and sleep.'

'Of course, by all means.'

Maria helped Jacob to the bedroom and sat by him until he fell asleep. Then she rejoined Heller.

'How is he?' he asked, with genuine concern.

'Sleeping.' There was a pause. 'So now you know our situation.'

'Yes.' Heller spoke without disguise. 'I am sorry, I didn't realise.' His apology trailed away.

'How could you? Everyone has a secret these days. It's the time of secrets, is it not, Herr Heller?'

'Yes.' There was no evasion in his answer. 'Yes, we all have our secrets.'

'Even you, I suspect.'

'Even me.'

In Maria's absence, Heller had cleared the table of the offending platters.

'Would you like a glass of wine?'

'Yes, yes I would, thank you, and a little cheese, if I may.'

'Of course. Please, be seated.'

The two sat opposite each other across the table. Maria touched an elaborately carved candlestick, one of a pair.

'These are beautiful,' she said.

'Thank you. They were an extravagance I permitted myself.'

'Then they are not family heirlooms?'

'No,' Heller said, with regret in his voice. 'I am afraid there is nothing of my family in these rooms.'

Maria nodded her understanding.

'It is difficult in these times to stay connected to your

past,' she mused aloud. 'May I light a cigarette?'

'Please, be my guest.'

Heller watched her intently as she took a lighter from her bag and held the cigarette between her rouged lips. He marked the way she threw her head back as she inhaled, and admired her throat and graceful neck. He studied her every movement. She closed her eyes and, holding the cigarette away from her face, slowly exhaled the smoke. She wore a sleeveless dress. Her long arms were smooth and finely shaped. Watching her, Heller let go of the caution he brought to his contact with people. He relaxed and waited until she came to attention from wherever she had been. Nor did he try to disguise the fact that he was studying her, admiring her.

Maria was not surprised or repulsed by his gaze. She smiled at him. 'It is good to smoke.'

There was another pause. She looked and leaned a little towards him across the table.

'What will you do with our secret, Herr Heller?'

'Keep it safe,' he replied, without hesitation.

'Yes, yes, I see that. Good. Thank you. I thought you would, though who can judge people when the times are so corrupt?'

'Things are complicated,' is all he ventured.

'And your husband?' he asked.

'Benjamin was arrested.' She did not elaborate.

'Why did you not leave, get out while you could?'

Maria laughed softly. 'Because we did not believe that these things would come to pass. In 1933, when they started introducing laws against us, my husband, Benjamin, stayed calm. He told his father that the laws were a ploy to garner support for the Nazis. He believed that once Hitler was securely in power, there would be need

114

for him to use the Jews. "The Jews," Benjamin used to say, "are Hitler's ladder. Once he's climbed to the top, the ladder will be of no more interest to him.""

Maria paused to draw on her cigarette. She continued, speaking quietly.

'The following year was calm and Benjamin believed that everything was going to work out. His father wasn't stupid, Herr Heller. He used his accountants and legal people to transfer ownership of his property to trusts and non-Jewish individuals. He dispersed his money over numerous accounts in Switzerland and here in Germany. We were never short of money. Benjamin's family had great wealth and with it we bought some freedom. And he had contacts. He knew whom to bribe. Nearly everyone has their price.' Maria stopped.

'Do you know what hurt him most, Herr Heller?' she asked, changing the direction of the conversation.

'No.'

'The law that forbade Jews to fly the German flag! My husband loved this country so much. "The Germans," he'd boast, "are the most rational people in the world." And then he'd declare, "This madness will soon end.""

Suddenly, she was sitting upright and speaking in a businesslike manner. 'Look at me, Herr Heller,' she commanded. 'What do you see?'

As she asked this question, she turned to and fro, holding her head in profile. 'Come on, tell me!' Her tone was ambiguous and playful, but aggressive too.

'A beautiful woman,' Heller answered, simply.

Maria laughed, surprised by the response.

'Thank you. A beautiful *Italian* woman,' she corrected, with a light note in her voice. 'Yes?'

'Yes,' he agreed, smiling at her.

115

But Maria's face twisted into a grimace. 'Well then you are a fool, Her Heller,' she announced with vehemence. 'Because I am a Jew! You see, I married a Jew. How simple it is! Is there anything as wondrous as Nazi rationality? I think not. My son, too, is a Jew, of course. He has to be. His father was a Jew. Do you admire the Nazi mind, Herr Heller?'

'To a point,' he replied, cautiously.

But Maria was not to be put off by his evasion. 'But surely not to this point? The point of no return. We have reached that point, haven't we?'

'I fear so.'

Maria sat back. 'I fear so, too.' She fell silent, smoking her cigarette. She cast an appraising look at the man opposite her. This stranger. He looked straight back at her.

'To the SS, of course, we – my son and I – are filth. It is not wise, Herr Heller, for you to meet with us, to invite us to your home, to fraternise with the enemy.'

Maria opened her hands in a gesture of appeal and explanation. 'But how could I refuse your invitation? I was afraid, you see – afraid that you might guess the truth and report us. And look, now here I am telling you everything. I need to trust in you, Herr Heller.'

Her tone grew defiant. 'You cannot live without trust. Perhaps I am a foolish woman, prattling on, indiscreet. Or maybe it is that I am tired. I know the end is near. And before it comes, I want to be myself for a few hours. I want to talk of my husband to someone. I want to be a woman talking to a man – mildly flirtatious, and trusting. Come what may of it.'

Heller made no reply.

'I know,' Maria continued, looking at the tablecloth,

where she traced a design with her finger, 'that you are not one of them. I don't know who you are, but you are not one of them.'

She raised her eyes, but he would not meet them.

They sat for a time, the flames of the candles dancing a little. Without a hint of self-consciousness, she resumed. 'Every night I wonder if they will come for us. But forgive me, you see I have forgotten how to talk to people. May I have more wine, please?'

Heller refilled her glass.

'This is good wine. It is some time since I sat at a table and drank wine and conversed. To your health, Herr Heller.'

They touched glasses.

She drank, allowing the wine to wash around her mouth.

'Of course, when the Nazis came to power,' she explained, 'things did not change overnight for us. We knew many people, people in government departments who had been dealing with the family firm for years, decades even. They were good, honest people. They liked and admired my husband's family. They helped us, inasmuch as they could.

'But by 1938, Benjamin knew that he had been mistaken. Things were not going to get better. My husband was a doctor. Did I mention that, Herr Heller?'

'No.'

'Yes, a doctor, a fine doctor. And then the government decreed that all Jewish doctors were forbidden to practise. Imagine! To be a doctor and be denied your right to tend the sick and the dying. Benjamin caught the smell of death in this decree. He didn't stop, of course. How could he? You see, because his family stayed, many people of his father's generation stayed too. Benjamin felt responsible. You raise your eyebrows, Herr Heller. You wonder, perhaps, how it was possible for a Jew to defy the laws?'

Maria laughed. She said with pride, 'Oh, my husband was a resourceful man. He bribed officials and SS officers. And he got results. His father had a large house on the outskirts of Berlin. Benjamin arranged for this to be listed as a private nursing home. He himself was the medical director. He gathered in seven of his parents' oldest friends. Forged documents gave them all new identities. Non-Jewish identities, naturally. Benjamin's Jewishness was conveniently forgotten by officials. Some because they knew and liked him. Others for the small fortune he paid them. And this house was a kind of haven.

'When the situation grew desperate, many came there to be treated or to seek comfort. The old, mainly, and the infirm. Oh, this husband of mine was brazen. You've no idea! He believed that those who accepted his money were trapped. But it wasn't all fear and self-interest. There were good people to help him. There is always decency, Herr Heller.'

Heller nodded and poured more wine. The wine was going to Maria's head. She talked more freely now. She was possessed by a compulsion to talk, to put the events of her history into a story that had a beginning, a middle and an end.

'But my darling Benjamin was racked with guilt. After '38 he knew that the talk of evacuating the Jews was a lie. He knew that those who boarded the evacuation trains would never return alive. He was well informed, you see. His main concern was to keep all knowledge of what was really happening from his parents. His mother and father were old. She was frail, semi-invalid. For them he had to be confident. To the German officials, he was full of bluster. And in his heart, in his frightened, gentle heart, he knew that it was useless.' As she spoke the last words, Maria's voice trailed away.

'How was he captured?' Heller asked.

'The rabbi, I think.'

Heller's eyes opened wide.

'Benjamin wanted his father and mother to have the comfort of the rabbi. So he brought him every week. The Gestapo may have trailed him. Who knows? My husband, that dear, good man, thought he had created an island. An enchanted island where the horrors of the time did not reach.'

Maria's words brought to Heller's mind the island of Hveen, where the astronomer Tycho Brahe had lived his idyllic life and observed the movement of the stars and planets before wanderlust and vanity sent him to Prague, to the court of Rudolf.

'Benjamin was like a little boy who believes in magic. Or a little boy who believes in his own cleverness. Funny, isn't it, Herr Heller, how, when all is lost, you cling to belief in yourself?'

'Often there is nothing else to cling to except self-belief and dreams.'

The two lapsed into their own thoughts.

'Then one day there was a call. A friend, perhaps, or someone on Benjamin's payroll? I really don't know. The voice on the other end of the line said, "Go. Go now. Benjamin is taken. They will soon be at your door. Fly." It was as simple as that. And though I had rehearsed this scene in my mind hundreds of times, when it was upon me I panicked. But we got away. Everything had been arranged. Dresden is an open city. It was not difficult to come here.

'Towards the end, when we were all together, we sang from the Book of Psalms. It comforted the old people. Benjamin did not want his mother and father to know the extent of the persecution or the number of their friends who had disappeared.

'And he hoped against hope that reason might prevail. That he would wake up one bright morning and the nightmare would be over. Every day he listened to the radio, waiting for the bulletin which would say, "Today, the government of the Third Reich is no more. Our country is free from their demonic tyranny."

'In his Jewish heart, I think he believed that the Messiah might come and save them.'

Heller nodded his understanding. They lapsed into silence again. At length Maria asked, 'Are you a religious man, Herr Heller?'

He shook his head. 'No.'

'You do not hate us, Herr Heller? You do not hate your Jewish guests, do you?'

He smiled his denial. 'You are welcome in my house.'

As he spoke, he reached his hand across the table and placed it gently on her bare arm. She covered his hand with her own.

'Thank you.'

In a low voice Maria began to sing:

Save me, O God, for the waters are come unto my soul.
I sink in deep mire, where there is no standing;
I am come into deep water, where the floods overflow me.
I am weary of my crying; my throat is dried; mine eyes fail
   while I wait for my God.

And as she sang, Herr Heller's voice was raised with hers:

Save me, O God, for the waters are come unto my soul.

*

Later, Heller wrote:

> They walked from the castle down Hradcany
> Hill to Mala Strana, to the house where Brahe
> had set up court. Kepler, impoverished and
> dependent, was forced to lodge there with his
> wife and child and his stepdaughter, Regina,
> whom he loved as his own. Jan joined the
> household for dinner. As always, Brahe kept a
> generous table. The meats were dressed with fruit
> sauces and cream, at the host's insistence, and
> there were ample supplies of sweet cake.

Heller reflected ruefully on the food shortage of the last
year. He was a man who enjoyed eating and deemed
himself a connoisseur of fine food. It gave him a peculiar
pleasure to visualise Brahe's table. Yet his own efforts to
provide a feast for Maria and her son had come down
around his ears.

> Jan, denied food in the White Tower, was ravenous,
> but the richness of the food made it almost
> indigestible and he left the table to throw up.
> Barbara, Kepler's wife, scowled and nagged
> at her husband for having taken on the res-
> ponsibility of a stray child while neglecting the
> welfare of his own family.

'Find us a home. Get us away from these people and demand from the emperor's pay-masters what is due to you. Then you can practise charity!'

Her whispered complaints were overheard by Brahe's dwarf, Jeppe, as he crouched at his master's feet. He stood on his footstool and sneered down the table.

'Master Mathematicus, go and wipe up your cur's dirt! And keep your woman under control! It is not fitting that a guest should insult my master's hospitality.'

Brahe laughed and rubbed some salve on the metal bridge of his nose. Brahe's son and a number of the assistants, jealous of Kepler, joined in the laughter.

'Mind your own dirt, you scurvy cur!' the host boomed, and he tossed meat to the floor, where, to Brahe's amusement, Jeppe pursued it like a dog.

Jan crept back to his place at the table, bewildered by the sight of the red-haired, hunch-backed dwarf, who was capering like a toy from the emperor's collection and competing with two large hounds for the scraps from Brahe's plate. He had escaped from one madhouse only to find himself in another.

Brahe turned on Kepler.

'Well, my half-cracked Lutheran, you will not waste my time or my money inventing fairy tales for Rudolfus Insanus. Cast a horoscope and tell his highness what it is he wants to know. And, by the Saviour's blood, it had better be convincing or you will be hanged in the town square while the emperor's officers stand by to gather the mandrake from under your gallows!'

Young Brahe seized his tankard and banged it on the table. 'Hang the Lutheran!' he screamed.

Jeppe joined in the shout and a great chorus of derision filled the hall.

Barbara glowered around the table at her husband's tormentors. 'Stop them,' she urged him.

Kepler's anger swelled within him. He turned on his wife. 'What will you have me do? Knock their heads together? Don't be stupid, woman!'

Barbara rose to her feet, tearful with frustration at the impotence of the lily-livered man who was her husband and burning with indignation that he should speak thus to her before these loathsome creatures.

'I will not spend another night under this roof,' she announced.

'Bravo, Mistress Barbara,' Brahe mocked. 'But where will you go? And what will you use for money? And where will you hide when the pestilence comes upon us?'

The laughter subsided. 'Here, at least, you have food and shelter,' he continued.

Barbara's rage died and she resumed her seat with a defiant look round the table.

'Is there talk of the plague?' Kepler enquired, anxiously.

'Yes,' Brahe said, simply. 'There are reports from the countryside. If the pestilence reaches the city, our emperor will lock himself in the deepest part of his citadel and not appear until the danger is past. And while the danger is present, your boy will be pressed to dream the future. And you, Kepler, will be kept busy casting his majesty's horoscope.'

'And what will the emperor demand of you?' Barbara asked, hatred and irony thickening in her voice.

'The elixir of life,' Brahe replied, and his sigh showed his weariness with the emperor's neurosis.

Kepler shifted uneasily in his chair. In dreams he had seen his body marked with livid crosses and he feared he would be struck down by the plague. The sores and infections he had suffered from boyhood convinced him that, in his case, putrefaction would be swift and terrible.

Barbara saw and understood the blanching of her husband's face.

'I fear, sir,' she said to Tycho, 'that your talk of the pestilence has upset my dear husband.' And she placed a solicitous hand on his head in a gesture of contempt and derision. Kepler brushed it away.

Heller rose from his desk. He was tired and drained from the effort of writing. He sat in an easy chair, Quince upon his lap, admiring in a vague, distant manner the assortment of shells and gemstones that formed his collection. His mind turned over the relationship between Kepler and his wife, Barbara. The astronomer's letters contained no hint of love or passion for her. Was their life together really the Punch and Judy affair he imagined it to be? Or did it suit his bachelorhood to construe it so? What would it be like to have a wife and child of his own? The prospect seemed remote and exotic but not unpleasant. He had never loved a woman before. Never possessed the courage to do so. Were the feelings he had for Maria the first stirrings of love? He was not sure. But he knew that he was not afraid. And her son, Jacob? That was a different matter. There was something in the boy – in all young boys, he suspected – that was cold and judgmental, that saw weakness and did not forgive it. He knew it would not be easy to face up to the boy's scrutiny. And thinking so, Heller fell wearily into his bed.

14

The Studio Of Raphael

Rome, 1512

The city stretched out before him. It was not far but, with only the protection of his woollen hose, walking was not easy. Andrea made his way to a track and hitched a lift with a farmer bringing chickens to the market. He sat alongside the old man as the cart rumbled its way to the city. To his relief, the farmer asked no questions and he rode silently into Rome in much the same manner as he had first arrived in Urbino. Overnight, the trappings of the court had been stripped away. Now, he had to rely on his own determination to succeed as an artist. Strangely, this thought filled him with a nervous exhilaration. Tattered and torn he might be, but he was, nonetheless, himself, Andrea Doni of Montecastelo. He had learned much in Urbino, but he was glad to be free of the restrictions and artificiality of the court. The sun shone, the little cart rumbled to the city and, while his head ached, his heart was light and free.

The farmer dropped him near the piazza of St Peter. He knew that Raphael's villa was in the vicinity of the square. The workshop, too, he thought. He made enquiries and found himself outside a house that might have belonged to a wealthy banker. It was four-square. The façade was unadorned, the main entrance plain and functional. Andrea hesitated, but only for a moment, and then made his way through the arched gateway.

He found himself in a courtyard. There was no one about. Uncertain what to do, Andrea walked under the arcade to his left and saw that its entire length housed the studio. Some boys worked preparing panels. He watched for a moment as they sanded the wood. One filled any holes or cracks with a mixture of sawdust and glue. Andrea knew that many coats of this gluey material would have to be applied and the wood scraped and sanded before it was deemed ready to receive paint. The boys worked, joked and talked easily among themselves.

Andrea entered the workroom and sought out the master. One of the boys, a bright, fair-haired youth, responded.

'Oh, our master is not here. He is with his master, Raphael, in the Vatican. He returns this afternoon.'

'But is Raphael not your master?' Andrea enquired.

'No, our master is Giovanni Udine.'

'I don't understand. Is this not the villa of Raphael Santi of Urbino?'

'Yes,' the youth replied, 'but there are many masters in the studio and the apprentices are assigned to them, not to Raphael. The masters are his assistants.'

'So how many are in the studio?'

The boy looked to his companions for confirmation, 'Forty?' he estimated. The others nodded. Andrea laughed.

'What is so amusing?' the boy asked, smiling.

'I have come to work in the studio. But I had visions of being Raphael's assistant. I find, I think, that I was mistaken.'

Now it was the boy's turn to laugh.

'I am here six months and I have not spoken one word to Raphael.'

Andrea held out his hand. He liked the open-faced youth, with his simple directness.

'I am Andrea Doni.'

The boy gripped his hand firmly. 'And I am Paolo Rossi. Come, let me show you around.'

Paolo showed Andrea the extent of the workshops. There were four rooms, chock-a-block with the folios of the students and masters. Colourful cartoons decorated the walls. There were canvases in various stages of completion, architectural models and figures sculpted in wax. None of these things was new to Andrea, but the sheer volume of work astounded him. Equally astonishing was the fact that, apart from the boys, there was no one about.

'But where is everyone?' Andrea asked. 'The studio is like a village that has been deserted.'

'Wait till this evening, when all are assembled to hear their instructions for the week to come. Then you will see the life that flourishes here. Signor Raphael has so many commissions that he runs from place to place. He even has an office and a smaller workshop within the Vatican itself.'

'Have you been there?'

'Yes.'

Andrea shook his head in disbelief.

'Come,' Paolo said, 'you must see my room. I am on the household staff. I am caretaker for the studio, so I sleep on the premises and eat with the other servants.'

He brought Andrea to a little cell-like apartment. There was a solitary window, high up, which admitted a burst of light. There was a simple mattress on the floor, a table and chair and a wash bowl. Behind the door was a small chest. On the walls were sketches and cartoons.

'Did you do these?' Andrea asked.

'Yes,' Paolo replied.

Andrea stepped towards one sketch. It showed a woman standing sideways in a rich gown, her face turned directly to the viewer. It was a strong, confident portrait. The gaze was bold and direct. He nodded his head.

'This is wonderful.'

'Thank you,' Paulo said, and the two boys' friendship was sealed.

The boys walked back towards the studio.

'And does Raphael live here?' Andrea asked.

'Of course. Along with Signora Margherita.'

'So he is married?'

'In a manner of speaking,' Paolo replied, laughing.

'How,' Andrea enquired, picking up on the playful tone, 'can one be married "in a manner of speaking"?'

'When the Pope talks of making you a cardinal, it is best not to have gone through a marriage ceremony. But rumours will not keep you warm at night in your bed. So Raphael and his beloved have not married, though they live as man and wife.'

'And is Raphael to be made a cardinal?'

'So it is rumoured.'

'And is his Margherita beautiful?'

'Some think so.'

'And you?'

'I know better than to have an opinion on Raphael's beloved. But come, you can see for yourself.'

And before Andrea had time to say anything else, Paolo was racing ahead up the staircase that led to the reception rooms of the villa. At the top of the stairs, he pulled the bell-rope, and the chimes sounded within. Presently, a young woman, not much older than the two youths, opened the door. Paolo bowed to her and held his hands across his heart in a gesture of earnest concern.

'I beg your pardon, Bianca. This young man has arrived looking for the master, Raphael, and there is no one to greet him or to receive him. And he has travelled a great distance and is tired and sore. Perhaps Signora Margherita can advise us what to do?'

Bianca, the mistress's friend and servant, considered Paolo with a knowing look.

'What game is this, Paolo?'

'No game, I assure you, good Bianca.' This was delivered with such sweet solicitude that Andrea emitted a laugh which he was forced to disguise as a cough. Bianca eyed him.

'Well, young fellow, have you no tongue to speak for yourself?'

Andrea looked at her, without shyness or embarrassment.

'Your master Raphael was in Urbino for the marriage of Elizabeth della Rovere and Bindo Gonzaga?'

The young woman nodded.

'While he was there, he met my master, Timoteo Viti, and saw samples of my work. Evidently he liked what he saw for he invited me to join his studio here in Rome. Last night, my belongings, including letters of greeting and commendations, were stolen from me by an itinerant group of players. Thus I arrive dishevelled and empty-handed. I assure you, however, that I am Andrea Doni of Montecastelo, courtier to Francesco, Duke of Urbino, and I received an invitation, in Raphael's own hand, to join this studio.'

As he introduced himself, Andrea made a formal bow that did justice to his tutor, Baldassare Castiglione.

Paolo was thunderstruck by the eloquence and self-possession displayed by his new friend, and Bianca too was taken aback. Most of the youths who came to the studio were shy, mumbling fellows, too much in awe to speak coherently. And Bianca, who was young, confident and beautiful, treated them with disdain. But it was she who curtseyed to Andrea and bid him and Paolo follow her. As she walked ahead, Andrea turned and winked at his friend, who gave him a thumbs-up salute. Bianca halted before a reception room and bid them attend her while she spoke to her mistress. She then returned, and the boys were ushered before Margherita Luni, daughter of a Roman baker, the woman whom Raphael loved.

The mistress of the house was dressed in a lavish gown of gold and ivory, with slashed sleeves that revealed the soft flesh of her upper arm. She sat on an upright chair but her whole body suggested ease and languor. Her hair was black, though largely hidden under a green and gold turban. She looked at the youths with a face that was kind, if detached and amused. She spoke softly and invited Andrea to repeat his story. Her voice was sweet and light and she spoke without affectation. So once again Andrea told his tale, embellishing it with colourful metaphors.

All the while he observed the lady. Her form was by no means perfect, according to the ideas of perfection he had been taught by Viti. Her shoulders were dropped and her neck lacked the long gracefulness that the painter considered an essential component of the ideal female form. Nor did her hands correspond to the rules of perfection. They were wide and strong, the fingers short and stumpy. And the line of her face, from ear to ear, was not clear and distinctive, as it ought to be. The chin was too pointed and the mouth was small, though expressive. In his mind, Andrea was making her portrait. He pondered the problem of doing justice to her eyes – which were large, magnetic and lovely – though he could not, as an artist, perceive what it was that made them attractive above other eyes. Yet for all the individual faults that he detected in her form, Margherita Luni was radiantly beautiful. Standing before her, reciting his story, Andrea decided that it was the graceful way that she inhabited her body and the unconscious lightness of her movement and gestures that made her beautiful – a beauty that no artist could capture unless he had the power to make moving images, to capture the play of her fingers on her arm as she listened to a boy tell his pretty tale for her amusement and pleasure.

'Ah,' she said, when he had finished, 'the voice and the face of an angel and the clothes of an urchin.'

Andrea blushed and the mistress laughed gently.

'You are a silver-tongued and amusing rogue, Master Doni, and I want you to tell me about the fine ladies of Urbino so that I might learn from their ways and improve myself.'

Now it was Andrea's turn to laugh, for never had he met someone who was so at ease with herself.

'Signora,' he replied, with no trace of flattery, 'you have nothing to learn from the court of Urbino.'

'Still, you must stay and amuse me and we shall dine together, and your scowling companion can stay too. But first we must get you properly dressed. Bianca, find some clothes for our guest, and see to a little food for the four of us.'

Thus it came about that Andrea Doni of Montecastelo

became a favourite of Mistress Margherita and, to the envy of every apprentice in the studio, got to wear a pair of ankle boots, a doublet and woollen hose from the wardrobe of Master Raphael. So the misfortune he suffered at the hands of the travelling players turned out to be the means by which he came to Raphael's attention and to the attention of Raphael's beloved, Margherita.

Compared to the other boys in the studio, Andrea was mature and accomplished beyond his years. The training in Urbino, and his work with Timoteo Viti, conferred inestimable advantages upon him. It was to Andrea that the other boys came seeking advice and help in all matters from painting to buying clothes. One lovesick apprentice even commissioned him to write a sonnet in praise of the girl who was the object of his affections. The poem did not succeed in wooing her but it was much admired by the youths in the studio, who borrowed the sestet for their own declarations of love:

Let him come no more to the streets of Rome
Who has no news of my darling beloved!
Even the smallest creatures of the golden earth
Can play in her garden and see my love
But I, love's fool, am banished from her sight.
Till there be remedy, I live in endless night.

Andrea was assigned to work with Giovanni Udine, who, along with Giulio Romana, collaborated with Raphael on many of his important commissions. Udine was a specialist in still life and in the painting of birds. He was responsible for the frieze in the frescoes painted by the studio – colourful garlands of luxurious fruits and flowers. He also had a genius for simulating the appearance of ancient marble.

Udine gave lessons in drawing. In these classes Andrea learned to look and examine the shape and texture of objects as he had never done before. So much did his master force him to concentrate on small details that he wondered if he had really seen the world up to now. True, he had always had a gift for reading a face, and his portraits were accomplished and insightful, but he had troubled himself less with noticing common objects in the world around him. Now all this had changed and his folios had drawings of various pebbles, a loaf of bread, his boot – anything, indeed, that came to hand. Every scrap began a source of wonder and interest.

The other youths recognised that Andrea was the most talented of the pupils and his work earned the praise of his master, Udine. Andrea was flattered by the invitation to lodge in the home of his master and took it as a sign of his artistic maturity, but Paolo warned him against this course of action, whispering of Udine's infamous reputation for pursuing young men.

At first, Andrea had thought his friend was joking, but it was not so. Through the good offices of Margherita, Raphael had agreed to the suggestion that Andrea share lodgings with Paolo. They were the only two apprentices who lived at Raphael's villa. The others lodged with the masters or with families in the neighbourhood. A small number lived with their parents. By staying at Raphael's villa, Andrea put himself outside the direct power of Udine and began to observe him closely.

He realised at once his good fortune in declining the invitation to lodge in the painter's house, for the master was a petty tyrant. He withheld money from the apprentices for no apparent reason, and his temper and affections were unpredictable. He was an elegant dresser and a fine conversationalist but he could also be crude and offensive. The apprentices had to take turns acting as a model for the life-drawing classes. Paolo had warned Andrea what to expect.

'In arranging a pose, he has a way of standing so close to you that you feel his breath upon your face. And he'll push against you till you can feel the pressure of his body against yours. *Sotto voce*, he makes improper suggestions and then laughs uproariously if you blush or show any signs of nervousness. When I posed for him, he held up my arm and pointed out its shape and structure to the students, and as he did so he ran his fingers over my skin in a way that made my flesh creep. Oh, he is one to watch!'

When Andrea's turn came, Udine wanted him to pose naked. This he refused to do, and when the older man tried to persuade and cajole him, touching his face and tousling his hair, Andrea pushed him away with a show of fierce indignation that put an end to the episode.

But in gaining a small victory, Andrea created a bitter enemy who made life as miserable as he could for the 'upstart from Urbino', as he called him. The tasks reserved for the most junior apprentice were given to Andrea, who had already served a year with Timoteo Viti and knew as much as any other boy in the studio. He swept the floor, cleaned brushes and palettes and sanded wood. He attended to these duties without complaint, though Udine contrived to find fault with everything he did. The fault-finding and carping were irritations but they did not, in truth, affect him. What was more difficult to endure was the fact that Andrea was not allowed to do any serious work. A number of the best apprentices were sent to help with the commission received by the studio from the banker Agostino Chigi to decorate the wall of an arcade in his villa that overlooked the Tiber. The prospect of working under the direction of Raphael filled Andrea with an unbearable excitement but, to his dismay, he was not chosen. And when, in class, he saw the preliminary sketches and the cartoon for the fresco, his disappointment and frustration turned to fury.

The painting was to be called *The Triumph of Galatea*. An apprentice asked Udine why it was so titled, and he explained that it portrayed the triumph of Galatea's beauty. Andrea knew that was not the case. Castiglione had spoken to him of platonic love and its symbols. Raphael's work depicted the triumph of the spirit over the senses. Thus it was that Galatea looked to the *putto*, half-concealed behind a cloud, who held his arrows in his hand. He symbolised platonic love. But it was pointless to contradict the master. Instead he set himself to studying the cartoon. The inspiration came from the story of the Cyclops, Polyphemus, who fell hopelessly in love with the beautiful Galatea and pursued her everywhere she went. Raphael portrayed the seaborne beauty in a shell chariot drawn by two dolphins as she made her flight from her unwanted suitor. The dolphins are guided by the boy-god Palaemon, who rescues sailors from storms and leads them through perilous seas. Galatea is accompanied by nereids and tritons, the sons and daughters of the sea-gods. Above their heads Cupid's *amoretti* make mischief with their arrows. Galatea, alone of the company, is unaffected and gazes steadfastly over her shoulder at the angel of spiritual love.

Andrea looked and took in the story and its symbolism. He then began to examine how Raphael had achieved the tremendous energy of the work while keeping Galatea as the centre of attention, despite the swirling movement all around her. How he envied Raphael's genius in creating these stretching, twisting, robust figures! And the colours – the dazzling, blinding blues and pinks and the magnificent imperial red of Galatea's cloak!

Oh, to see the master at work as he applied the paint quickly and precisely! And though Andrea knew that the apprentices would do no more than mix plaster and wash brushes or hold the ladder, to see and be near Raphael would be an education in itself. But no! He, Andrea Doni, who understood the meaning of the painting better than any of the boys and masters in the studio, was forced to stay behind and sand wood! Andrea, raging, angered, self-pitying and powerless, bolted from the studio, raced up the staircase and sounded the chimes on the door of Raphael's apartments. He knew that the master was not there but he needed to pour out his heart and his grievances and he knew that Margherita would listen and understand. And, maybe, speak to her beloved for him.

So, when Bianca led him to her mistress, he launched forth in a flood of complaint, indignity and frustration. To his surprise, he concluded his speech with a paean to Baldassare Castiglione. And when the words came to an abrupt halt and he stood, trembling and shame-faced, before the mistress of the house, she rose, raised his face, placed a gentle kiss upon his lips, held Andrea close and waited for the tears of passionate self-pity that she knew would come.

15

Final Journey

Dresden, Summer 1995

Jacob Philip and his grandson, Ben, are leaving Dresden, travelling on a night train to Italy. Though they wandered here and there in the city, they did not find Heller's apartment. And Jacob's mood grew remote and dark. He lies now sleeping, or so Ben assumes. Out of the silence, he asks, 'Do they still teach you grammar in school, Benjamin?'

Ben, accustomed to his grandfather's unpredictability, responds casually, 'Not much, Grandad. Just a little in French. Tenses and things like that.'

'The past, the present, the future. Grammar makes everything so simple, doesn't it? But it's not really like that. Some things have no end. The last time I left this city, for example. That day, that journey.'

*

Maria is standing at the table in the kitchen putting out dishes for breakfast. She senses the soldier's presence before she sees him and understands who he is. He is young – not much more than twenty. A new recruit, untried in battle and afraid.

'Frau Philip?' he asks, with forced conviction.

Maria stands for a moment, almost amused, before replying, 'Yes, I am Maria Philip.'

'You must come now, you and your son.'

Jacob is sleeping, the covers pulled high around him. Maria stands looking down at him before she shakes him awake.

'They have found us, my love. You must dress quickly. Put on your warm clothes.'

He sits up, reassured by his mother's calm air. And then the soldier is in the room.

'Quickly now,' he orders, waving his rifle, and ushers them out of the house.

They are brought to a police barracks outside Dresden. In the morning, after a night in the cell, a sergeant comes and gives them coffee and a filled pastry. They eat because they are cold.

'Because it is good to eat,' Maria says. 'We will need our strength.'

An SS officer arrives. He exchanges some jokes with the sergeant. The cell door is opened and they are brought out. All the while, the two men continue their conversation. In the pauses between laughter and hilarity, they are told what to do.

They are transported to a place deep in the countryside where railway lines converge and multiply. They stand and wait as their two guards smoke and chat a short distance away from them.

An SS car – the familiar black Mercedes – arrives on the scene. The officer gets out and approaches the group. Almost at once, the soldiers lose their casual air. The officer looks at them and a smile forms on his lips. Encouraged, Jacob asks, 'Where are we going, sir?'

But he has misread the smile. The officer takes one step forward and strikes him hard with his open palm on the side of the face. He cries out, more in astonishment than in terror, and Maria throws her arms around him, shielding him from any more blows. But no more come. The officer stands impassively. There seems to be no connection between him and the blow that he has struck.

'You must be silent.'

This is all. Presently another truck arrives and three prisoners, spent and lifeless, are led past them down the track. After a time a train draws near. They hear the screech as the brakes engage and the hissing of steam. The track vibrates, the tremors reaching to where they stand. The train has many trucks – the cattle trucks spoken of in whispers. When it shudders to a halt, a truck door is before them. This is the worst moment: the door before them. They know what it means.

They stand at the side of the tracks feeling beaten and empty. The SS officer steps forward and unlocks the door. He pulls it back. A rush of fetid air hits them. Jacob draws back but a guard pushes the length of a rifle across his back and prevents any further recoil. They stand for some moments looking at the pathetic, huddled figures within. The light dazzles them. They blink. Jacob sees the faces. Most dull with stupor. Some fearful and afraid. One or two eager and hopeful. Faces from a twilight world. Faces from the edge of a canvas.

Maria smiles uncertainly at the faces before her. But the occupants of the truck are too dispirited and tired to respond. Some have been in the truck three days, transported from the south of France. They have received water and some bread each day. A corner of the truck has been heaped with straw and serves as a latrine. For two days, the contents were swept out each time the door was opened. But now people are too apathetic to make the effort. Maria and Jacob are rooted to the spot. The guards push them forward with the butts of their rifles. And then the officer speaks.

'Your coat, please. Quickly, your coat.'

And when Maria looks uncomprehendingly at him, he reaches forward to remove it from her shoulder. She, mistaking his gesture, moves to avoid the blow she thinks is aimed at her. She stumbles and loses her footing. Jacob cries out in protest and moves to help her but a guard pushes his rifle into his chest and he falls against the truck. Maria rises and removes the coat. She hands it to the officer, who thanks her politely. Without taking his eyes from her, he says, 'And the boy's.'

Jacob obeys, meekly. Then they are pushed and shoved into the dark interior and the door is dragged closed behind them.

They fall onto people huddled on the floor. Some groan. One figure lashes out with his boot. Somehow, a space opens and Maria finds herself sitting on the soiled and damp straw with her back against the wall of the carriage. Jacob sits close to her. He lets her put her arm around him. The train begins to move slowly but, almost as soon as it begins, it comes to a halt. Then the first of many silences begins. The train stays put. Maria asks quietly, 'What is happening?' No one responds. To ask questions is a sign of innocence or stupidity. The waiting continues; the foul air clogs their lungs and the damp of the straw seeps into their limbs.

Without warning, the door is pulled back. Sunlight floods the small space. Its sudden presence is alarming and dazzling. A guard passes up and down. A child, wrapped in a blanket which conceals a bundle of bank-notes, is handed forward. The guard, checking all round to ensure he is unobserved, takes the child and reads the note attached to the clothing: 'Please save my baby. May God bless you.'

Maria and Jacob are near the door. After a time they pluck up the courage to sit with their legs dangling over the side. The breeze catches their hair. They take off their shoes and socks and wiggle their toes. The breezes brush their ankles and insteps. There are trees, tall and slender, near the tracks. The branches rock and sway as the wind catches them. There is birdsong. The twittering of a small flighty thing and the sustained whooping of another, larger bird. It is hard to imagine the fantastic journey that has been interrupted. But the interlude comes to an end. Doors are fastened. The light is locked out.

At last the train begins to move and pulls out of the siding onto the main track. As it gathers speed, the pistons beat out a rhythm and the wheels strike sparks off the tracks. And the truck, with its cargo of Jews, swings and sways its way towards the east.

The journey continues through one night. There are many stops. Each time the train shudders to a halt there is a rustling in the carriage and the air tenses with expectancy. Maria settles Jacob's hair and brushes the dust from his clothes. Ordinary motherly acts that she performs without thinking. And when nothing happens, people settle again. Though the night is long, there is little rest. The carriage is stuffy and there are people tossing and turning. Curses and irritated shouts follow as someone turns and bumps against someone else. Many in the truck know that the journey will end in darkness, yet they complain, as they have always done in life. Not even the approach of death can shake them free of habit.

The noises of the carriage scramble around Jacob's head, growing in intensity until he think his ears will burst or he will scream out in despair. And always, as the noises reach their terrible pitch, Maria soothes him with soft words and hugs him close to her like a baby. And then he finds a little peace. Once he closes his eyes and dozes, and for the briefest time he is immortal and panthers lick his outstretched fingers.

Towards evening, the train arrives at its destination. The door is flung back and the carriage illuminated by the dazzling light of ark lamps. Some brave souls lean their heads out of the truck to see what is happening. One is a youth, not much older than Jacob. A soldier hits him full in the face with the butt of his rifle, snapping his head back. He falls lifeless into the truck. There is little panic. People withdraw into themselves, to a place which cannot be reached. All wait. An officer appears. He gives orders in a clear, strong voice.

'Follow instructions. It is imperative that order be maintained,' he insists. 'Men and boys over fifteen will assemble on the platform at the right-hand side, ahead of the train. Women and children to the left. Leave all luggage and personal possessions in the truck. These will be returned to you at a future time.'

The evacuees bestir themselves. There is a subdued hum of conversation. Among the family groups, husbands and wives embrace. There are some tears, but the passengers know so little of their fate that all feelings are buried. Some hide wallets and other valuables in their clothing or in their shoes.

On the platforms, SS officers move among them. Men

are quizzed on their age and state of health. They are then sent to a convoy of waiting trucks or directed further along the platform towards the entrance to a camp of some kind. No selection is made among the women and children. All are directed towards the camp.

By and large the scene is strange but not violent or confused. The officers are unfussed, professional. Asked by a young woman when she will see her husband again, an officer replies, 'Soon. You will all be together again soon. There's no need to worry.'

As the line of evacuees forms, orderlies approach the trucks and begin sorting out luggage. They are grotesque figures – human scarecrows in filthy, striped rags. Their hair is cropped and they shuffle like mechanical toys. They do not look at or address the new arrivals.

Across on the men's side, one man breaks from the line and makes off into the darkness. An arc light is turned on him and a pair of dogs set off in pursuit. The men are told not to look but to continue making their way forward. But not even the strains of a Mozart tune filling the night air can hide the fearful screams of the escapee as the dogs fall on him.

And even as they shuffle forward in the line, Maria and Jacob think themselves fortunate. After all, they have each other. They are not pitiful or contemptible. Jacob sees that his mother is still beautiful. True, her eyes are sad and her face is pale and drawn, but she has the beauty of Raphael's Madonna, the beauty of someone who has seen and felt great pain but who can look out on the world without flinching. And, they remind themselves, they are together. Jacob might well have been sent to the men's camp. He is a borderline case, but their good fortune holds. The officer agrees to Maria's plea to allow her to keep her boy. 'Yes, yes, it is good for a son to be with his mother,' he says. And, feeling grateful for every kindness, Maria thanks him fervently.

Yes, how fortunate they are among the wretched. And then there is a change. For now the line of guards usher them along with greater urgency, dogs bark and snarl and people stagger as a rain of blows falls on them. And still Jacob tries to smile, tries to believe in their good fortune. Though he is trying to be manly, he starts to cry. And then they are herded into a room with hundreds of others. Guards shout and order them to strip. Many are shamed by their nakedness and seek to hide it, and then they are all driven, like cattle, towards the shower room. As the doors are sealed and the jets turned on, Jacob prays, 'Guardian angel be near me!'

But it is water, not gas, that rains down upon them. Blessed, cold water that stings the skin with its sharpness. Maria and Jacob exchange looks of astonishment and disbelief. And then they hug each other close and would, certainly, have collapsed if they had not been packed in so tight. And there is a great wailing and screaming and crying. Fear and terror and relief, all in one.

*

'The time after that is all a blur,' Jacob tells Ben. 'We lived in the camp. For a time we tried to hold on to our dignity, our sense of privacy. But you cannot do that when people are so close to you that you no longer know the odour of their bodies from that of your own. Sometimes we got little treats or periods of respite. One guard said we owed these to our friend in the ministry. Mother believed it was Herr Heller. I don't know. I tried to contact him after the war. It is thought that he died in the great fire that destroyed Dresden in the spring of 1945.'

'Do you remember much about the camp?'

'No. Most of it I don't want to remember. I do recall my dreams. Or one dream that recurred. Don't ask me why, but I do.'

'A dream?'

'In the camp I had the strangest dream. A fantastic, exhilarating dream. I dreamt of Africa. Of wide, wide spaces, with the shadow of mountains in the distance. And wild animals. As a child, I always loved wild animals. Dreamt of being a wolf-boy, surrounded by animals who did my bidding.'

Ben twists himself so that he is hanging over the side of his bunk looking in on his grandfather, puzzlement written over his features.

Jacob opens his eyes wide with a 'Don't-ask-me-to-explain' look on his face.

There is a moment's quiet as Jacob returns to the dream and Ben tries to imagine it. At length he objects, saying, 'But you've never been to Africa, Grandad.'

'No.'

'So how did you know what to dream?'

Jacob laughs. 'I must have lived there in a previous existence!'

Ben looks at the dark ceiling of the carriage. He shakes his head. The rhythm of the train fills the compartment. There is a muffled cough from somewhere down the carriage.

He asks in a quiet voice, 'Did you spend long in Auschwitz, Grandad?'

'No. After six weeks or so, I was sent to Terezin with

some other children. It was better there. We went to school. The paintings and poems we saw in the Pinkas Synagogue were made there. Franz Heller, I believe, arranged for me to go. But mother had to stay behind in the camp. I didn't know, of course. I thought she'd be transferred too.'

Ben is trying his best to say the right thing, knowing he is getting into deep waters.

'It must have been hard, being separated from her.' A moment's anxiety. Relief when grandfather's voice carries up to him.

'To begin with, it wasn't. You see, during my time in Terezin I had vivid pictures of her. It was as if I could see all that was happening in the camp I'd left behind.'

Ben, trying to ease his own tension. 'Grandad, if I didn't know you better, I'd say you were cracking up.'

Laughter. 'No. There's no fear of that. But your mind works differently, Benjamin, when each moment is touched by death. I did see those visions.

'One showed a musical gathering in the commandant's house. The wives of the officers were all there in evening dresses. Their hair was braided and coiffured into elegant shapes. A fire burnt in the grate. At a grand piano a woman sang Schubert songs to her own accompaniment. The faces of the gathering were directed towards her. Mother was in the room. She was wearing the striped garments of the inmates. She wore a small scarf but it was clear that her hair had been cut. She moved among those people carrying coals to rekindle the fading fire. But no one saw her. She was a ghost among them. Departing the room, she hesitated for a moment and savoured the songs she herself had sung. Her face was beautiful but they did not see her. I hated them for that.'

Ben refrains from any comment.

'There were others. Mother in the commandant's office, cleaning, wearing her scarecrow outfit, dusting a photograph of the commandant's two boys. She smiles at it in the way a mother smiles at photographs of children. I want to shout at her. I don't want her touching it. Behind the desk hangs a framed piece of embroidery.' Jacob's voice quivers with indignation. 'Do you know what it says? "A day is beautiful when it is touched by kindness."'

'In the last vision I had of her she was in a garden. The boys from the photograph were playing there. The walking scarecrows who came sometimes to their house were so strange that they were not even touched by curiosity. They accepted them as they accepted the existence of daddy-long-legs and other fantastic creatures. These creatures tottered and staggered. They blinked stupidly and had not, it seemed, the gift of speech. They were not to be touched. They were dirty and repulsive.

'The two boys, with soft flesh and blue eyes, were playing in the garden. It was hot, so they were wearing short trousers and nothing else. Their bodies were like the *putti* of a Renaissance painting.

'My mother saw the boys and was taken by their stance. One held a long stick, like a javelin, above his head. His arm was braced, ready to hurl the missile. The other stood at a right angle to his brother, his arms resting on the other's shoulder. Both looked ahead to where a bird searched for worms.

'The sun was dazzling. The scene was picturesque. My mother stood to observe the children. They didn't see her. When the boy threw the spear and the bird scrambled away to safety, she laughed a light, musical laugh.

'The boys heard it. They turned and smiled. Her

laughter and their smiles joined for the briefest moment. But then the world intervened between them. The boys frowned and my mother, the scarecrow, hurried back to her world.'

Silence fills the carriage. Ben does not know how to respond. Jacob resumes.

'And then the visions stopped coming to me. And when they stopped I knew that she was dead.'

'You've never told me these stories before.'

'I don't think I have told anyone these stories, Benjamin.'

Ben understands that a compliment has been paid. 'Thank you,' he says. As an afterthought, he adds, 'Do you have a real photograph of your mother, Grandad?'

'Yes.'

'May I see it, please?'

Jacob lights the lamp above his head. He removes the small photograph from a breast pocket. He hands it up to Ben, who is in the couchette above him.

It is a small studio portrait of a young woman's head. She wears a white lace collar. Her head is tilted to the left. The eyes stare into the middle distance away from the lens. She has a distant look – not dreamy, almost a frown. Her black hair is combed tightly to her head and gathered behind. Her mouth is full. Her neck long and graceful. The jawline strong. Maria is beautiful, though her expression is severe.

Light-hearted, Jacob asks, 'What do you think? Isn't she beautiful?'

Ben replies honestly, without guile, 'No, not really.'

Both laugh.

The photograph is handed back. Jacob places it carefully in his breast pocket. He rarely looks at it. It is the feel of the paper that he responds to. This fragment of the past that has survived intact. Jacob thinks its survival is miraculous. The flimsy piece of paper has moved beyond its past – outgrown it, like a sacred relic whose power is only vaguely connected to its starting point. Jacob clutches it to his heart as he falls asleep on a night train bearing him and his grandson to Italy.

In the early morning, when Ben wakes, he pulls the curtains. Outside is a world of green. Villages on mountainsides with tall, slender campaniles surveying the countryside around. Cypress trees, oak and Spanish chestnut, umbrella pines and olive trees. The rich luxury of the Italian countryside, the countryside of his great-grandmother.

16

VISIONS OF ANGELS

Rome, 1512–13

Word, alarming and exciting, came to Andrea that his master, Raphael, required him to be ready at sunrise to accompany him to the Vatican for an audience with Pope Julius to discuss the commissioning of an altarpiece for a church in Piacenza. Bianca, the bearer of the news, had been instructed to ensure that Andrea acquired whatever new clothes he needed for this occasion.

'But what does it mean, Bianca?' Andrea asked.

'It means that Margherita whispered to her love and he promised to make you his assistant on his next commission. So be ready at sunrise!' Seeing the startled, bemused look on Andrea's face, Bianca laughed and kissed him. And the pair set off to buy the clothes that Andrea would wear in his audience with Julius.

It was not a long walk from the studio to the Vatican. Raphael put him at his ease. It was like the old days with Baldassare Castiglione. His former teacher had maintained that the time spent going from one place to another should never be wasted. So when his new master asked if Andrea was making good progress in his studies, the young man did not give the polite answer that was expected.

'No, sir, I cannot in truth say that I am making progress.'

Raphael was surprised by this – taken aback, even.

'Why, what is the matter, Andrea?'

'Well, it is true that my skill in drawing has improved. Certainly I have learned to look on the world with the eyes of a stranger. And for this, sir, I am grateful.'

'But?'

'But the hand is only an instrument of the mind. Unless the mind is nurtured, the artist will remain childlike.'

Raphael looked with interest at this new assistant. 'Is there not enough happening in the studio to stimulate the mind?'

'I do not think so, sir.'

'No?' There was a note of genuine surprise in the master's voice.

'No.' Andrea spoke with clarity and purpose. 'We, the apprentices, are too isolated and too much in our own company. There is little we can teach each other. We need your guidance, sir.'

Raphael, gentle and considerate as he was, was not used to criticism, implied or direct. He struggled to formulate a response. 'I do not have the time, Andrea, to teach you. As it is, we have to turn down work. Moreover, I am a painter, not an educator. I run a studio, not, alas, an academy.' At this point his tone grew decisive. 'Besides, it is the duty of my assistants to instruct you. Surely you have learned from them?'

'Oh yes, sir, many things. I have learned not to give offence and to keep my opinions to myself. And I have learned my powerlessness.'

Raphael did not reply at once, and when he spoke it was as if he was thinking out loud. 'It may be that I have had too little care for you all, but I am away a great deal of the time. It is not possible.'

They were now approaching St Peter's Square. The early-morning traffic of people and goods had begun. Andrea knew that he would not have Raphael's undivided attention for much longer. He was not going to squander this opportunity.

'I know, sir, that the demands upon your time and genius are great. Perhaps, however, Mistress Margherita could supervise the education of the apprentices? The great minds of Rome come to the villa but they pass us by. Sometimes, in my despair, I think we are no better than the horses left outside in the street munching oats, while inside, their masters engage in sweet discourse.'

Raphael laughed and placed a comforting arm around Andrea's shoulder.

'Surely things are not quite so bad?'

'You do not know, sir, how bad they are!'

There was a silence. Andrea was apprehensive. Perhaps he had said too much. Perhaps he had offended the master. He greeted Raphael's reply with relief.

'What would you have taught to the boys?'

'The ancient writers, philosophy and mathematics. These for a start.'

'Why these?'

Now Andrea was deep within his own thoughts, eager and bright.

'I want, sir, to be as great an artist as you. So do all the boys in the studio. But we will never be great unless our minds are sharp and filled with knowledge. Greatness is a matter of mind. Turn your studio into an academy!'

Raphael laughed.

'You are nothing if not persistent, Andrea, and there

is merit in your arguments. I do not deny that. But I do not have the time to run an academy *and* a studio. It is simply not possible.'

'Forgive me, sir, I think you are mistaken.'

'Were you not so well-spoken and courteous, Andrea, I would say that you are impertinent! How, pray, am I mistaken?'

'I think, sir, that you could become the Socrates of Rome. Let your students gather around you as you make your way through the city. Think how much you could teach as you walked from the villa to the Vatican! And there is the example of Aristotle, who taught as he walked, with his students trailing after him. I believe, sir, though I have not seen it, that your *School of Athens* pays homage to these great teachers.'

'Andrea, you have been well schooled by my friend, Baldassare, for I have never encountered so fresh-faced a youth with such powers of persuasion and flattery. I promise to think on what you have said. And in a little time you can see for yourself my Plato, Aristotle and Socrates.'

'Thank you, sir.'

In the company of Raphael, it seemed the most natural thing in the world to enter the Vatican, take the salute of the Swiss Guard and walk in the loggia leading to the Pope's suite of rooms. The Pontiff was in the central chamber in his apartments – his private library – working at his writing desk, attended by his secretary. Raphael and Andrea stood in the doorway, waiting for Julius to see them and summon them to him. The pause gave the youth time to survey the room. He looked to the ceiling, dwelling on the winged figure of Poetry, surrounded by angels bearing inscriptions from Virgil's *Aeneid*. His eye was then drawn to the dramatic depiction of the Judgement of Solomon, painted against a background of gold mosaic. Raphael enjoyed observing his young assistant react to his work.

Andrea, for his part, was filled with wonder, pleasure and disbelief at the beauty and power of the frescos. Then his eyes fastened on the *School of Athens*, which filled the wall behind Julius's desk. In his excitement, Andrea grasped Raphael's arm and exclaimed, 'Oh! Look!'

His master gave a gentle laugh. The Pope looked up from his work and waved them in. Raphael knelt and kissed Julius's ring and introduced Andrea, who also knelt and paid his respects.

'Where are you from, my child?' the Pontiff asked, with a meekness that belied the strength and forcefulness of his character.

'Montecastelo, Holy Father.'

'It is a village outside Urbino,' Raphael explained, adding, 'Andrea has been educated by no less a personage than Baldassare Castiglione, at your nephew's court.'

'Indeed,' said the Pontiff, looking directly at Andrea. 'Then you are a fortunate youth. Is he a kind and virtuous boy?' the Pontiff asked Raphael.

'Virtuous and with more ideas than ten of his age,' Raphael replied with affectionate good humour, and Julius, in turn, smiled.

After the pleasantries, the Pontiff spoke of the commission.

'I have lately received a delegation from the city of Piacenza. The city swears its allegiance to Rome and to me. As a mark of my favour, I wish to make a gift of an altarpiece for the church of St Sixtus, which is currently being restored. It is my intention to reconsecrate the church on completion of the work. You will paint this for me?'

'Your Holiness, it is always an honour to work in your service.'

'Good, good,' the old man replied, and his eyes wrinkled into a smile.

It was nine months since Andrea had seen Julius at Urbino. He was shocked by the extent to which the Pope had aged and grown frail in that time. The Holy Father had contracted malaria and had almost died. Undeterred by his ill health, he took on a gruelling workload that involved not only fighting the French but also calling a council of the Church. The military campaign had come perilously close to ruination and, for a time, it seemed that his enemies might drive him from Rome. And though he had triumphed, the effort and the sickness had drained him. Seeing the haggard look of his face, Andrea knew that the Pontiff had not much time left on this earth. The thought chilled him and he gave an involuntary shudder.

'You sang for me, at the wedding of my grand-niece Elizabeth to Bindo Gonzaga?'

Andrea was startled. 'Yes, your Holiness,' he replied.

'See, I am not as close to death and forgetfulness as you imagine I am.'

Andrea could not control the blush that rose on his cheeks. A vague terror gripped him that Julius could read all his thoughts. His confusion caused Julius to laugh.

'Your master tells me that you will be his assistant, so listen well to my instructions.'

The laughter was still in the Pope's voice, but there was also the force of authority that brooked no contradiction.

'I want a portrait of the Virgin, with St Sixtus and St Barbara in attendance, for relics of the two saints will be housed in the church. Furthermore, I want the painting to be done on canvas so that it might be borne in procession before me as I go to say Mass in the city.'

'As you wish, your Holiness.'

'When will you commence work?'

'Almost at once. I will work here in the Vatican, in my workshop, so that you may, if you so desire, monitor the progress of the painting.'

'Very good. My secretary has prepared a contract. Return to me if it is not to your satisfaction.'

The Pontiff extended his hand and Raphael kissed the ring. The interview was over.

The months which followed were among the happiest of Andrea's life. He was sixteen years old and working with Raphael Santi on a commission for the Pope. His job was to ensure that the workshop had everything that his master might need and to keep the working space clean and uncluttered. Raphael was the gentlest of men but he was an exacting artist and accepted nothing less than the best from his assistants. Andrea's one aim was to please him. Within weeks his admiration for his master had grown to devoted loyalty. When he worked on preparatory sketches and studies, Raphael did so in complete silence – the absorbed silence of intense concentration that tightened the muscles of his youthful face and narrowed his eyes. Otherwise, he was talkative, sharing his ideas with his young assistant.

'The figure of St Sixtus must bear the likeness of Julius. We will show him interceding with the Virgin for the faithful. Therefore we must capture in his face a sweetness of mind. I have an idea, Andrea, to have Julius drawing the Virgin's attention to those who kneel before the altar. This way, everyone who looks upon the painting will think that it is for them that their Pontiff speaks to Mary.'

Another day he exclaimed, 'The Virgin must be painted so that it seems she walks towards the congregation. They will think that she is about to step into their church!' For every idea, Raphael wrote a note and made preliminary sketches. As part of the preparation and planning, models were brought into the studio. Raphael wanted, in particular, to observe the fall of the garments as they posed for him. But the face of the Virgin was, Andrea knew, modelled on the face of Margherita. In the sketches, the Virgin stepped forward, the movement of thigh and knee clearly visible beneath her robe, as a gust of wind swelled her gown and veil. The pose suggested movement – the sweet gracefulness that Andrea had seen in Raphael's beloved.

He studied the expression on the Virgin's face for a long time. She had the countenance of one who looks upon what she would rather not see. It was the startled look of a tender heart. What she saw made her hold her babe close to her. His round, staring eyes were filled with fright and he inclined his head towards the safety of his mother, his left hand catching hold of his right ankle as he looked out at the world. The mother's long fingers were soft against the tender flesh of her child. Andrea was put in mind of Margherita's habit of running her fingers over her upper arm, and he saw the gesture transformed in the painting. Andrea loved the way his master had drawn the Virgin's feet – real feet that trod the clouds and carried her towards this world of ours.

Some days Andrea was alone in the workshop, cleaning, tidying, storing or sketching. On more than one occasion the Pontiff came to view the work in progress. He sat examining the sketches Andrea laid before him, saying little. It pleased Andrea to be able to play a small part in the old man's life, for he grew more certain that Julius was dying. The interludes in the workshop, studying the tender face of Raphael's Virgin, were part of his preparations for the journey into death and brought, Andrea suspected, a quietude to his soul. Between the old man and the youth there was a sympathy that needed no words.

There were other visitors. Baldassare Castiglione, visiting the Papal court, came and took his protégé to lunch in a neighbouring eating house. The occasion was joyful and celebratory. Michelangelo, too, called into the workshop. His reputation suggested that he was difficult, quick to take offence and so fearsome that even the Pope dared not cross him. Andrea stayed out of his way and observed him closely. The creator of the *Pieta* was muscular and wiry, with dark, thick hair and a sparse beard. In his rough woollen tunic, he looked like a labourer. His eyes were sharp and piercing, and his bearing suggested the pent-up energy of a wild cat.

The exchanges between him and Raphael were polite, but Andrea saw the suspicion in the older man's attitude to his master when Raphael enquired about the progress of work in the Sistine Chapel. Michelangelo's eyes blazed, and he answered in a cautious manner that gave nothing away.

As the year progressed, the work took shape. By autumn Raphael was ready to begin painting the canvas. Even as he started, the scaffolding was taken down in the Sistine Chapel and thousands of Romans crowded in to see the astonishing, brilliant masterpiece created by the restless, fiery little man. Julius was delighted with Michelangelo's achievement and, though there was no comparison in the scope of the work, Raphael hoped to give him equal pleasure with his painting.

The figure of St Sixtus was painted first. Wrapped in a golden-ochre cope, he gazed lovingly at the Virgin, his left hand across his heart, his right pointing to the congregation. A breeze from below caught the end of his great cloak. The face of this soul in bliss bore the unmistakable features of Julius, softened and made tender by the presence of the Queen of Angels. The Pontiff came and was gratified.

'Yes,' he said, 'soon I will be kneeling at the foot of the Virgin. I am not afraid to die, Raphael. I have fought for God and would go now to my eternal rest.'

Raphael worked quickly, seeking to grant Julius his wish of seeing the work completed before his death. The figure of St Barbara was added, kneeling on the opposite side of St Sixtus. She genuflects, her eyes averted from Mary and the Infant. She is graceful and reverent.

And, as the painting came to life on the canvas, the life faded from Julius. He praised each new development and urged Raphael to press ahead. By Christmas Eve, the Pope felt so weak that he called to be anointed with holy oils. Unexpectedly, Andrea received a summons from the Papal apartments to attend the Pontiff. He was ushered in, and Paris de Grasis, the chief of protocol, advised the youth that Julius wished to hear him sing some of the

Songs of David. A book of words and music was given to him and de Grasis brought him into the Pope's private chamber. The Pontiff sat propped in a high chair, a blanket over his knees. His body seemed lost in the cloak that surrounded it. Julius did not open his eyes, and his words came from his mouth in the merest whisper.

'Is the boy here?'

'Yes, your Holiness.'

'Good. Page forty-five. Sing for me, boy, if you will.'

Paris de Grasis signalled that Andrea should do as he was bid. He opened the hymnal and sang with all his heart:

Save me, O God, for the waters are come unto my soul.
I sink in deep mire, where there is no standing;
I am come into deep water, where the floods overflow me.
I am weary of my crying; my throat is dried;
Mine eyes fail while I wait for my God.

When he had finished, Julius opened his eyes, though Andrea doubted whether the Pope saw anything in this world. However, the image of the thin, pinched face staring into the distance stayed with him as he hurried back to the studio.

Raphael toiled without cease, working now on the figure of the Madonna. As she appeared on the canvas, she was as beautiful and as gentle, as corporeal and as real as she had been in the sketches. She stepped forward from behind the veil of heaven into our world. Her face possessed more sweetness and suffering than Andrea believed it possible to convey.

To heighten the apparitional effect of the painting, Raphael decided to add curtains in the top right- and top left-hand corner of the canvas. Now, more than ever, the Virgin seemed to step towards the spectator. All that remained was to paint the billowing clouds, for the master had elected to eliminate the usual architectural elements from the background. Andrea was entrusted with this task as Raphael gave the final touches to the figures.

The master required a plain white background for the upper portion of the painting – more mist, indeed, than cloud. But as Andrea worked, he began to experiment. Through the mist, at the edge of the canvas and bordering the curtains, he sketched shadowy faces. Faces watching the Virgin's progress. The faces were not the usual cherubim blending with the clouds of heaven. No, they were something more indistinct and ambiguous. Mysterious – sinister, even. Some of the childish faces displayed fear and some were crying. They were the faces of lost, frightened children. Where they had come from Andrea did not know, but he worked with an instinctive feeling for their rightness. He was certain, yet he was shy. What if his master did not want him to continue? He dared not risk his master's opinion, so he said nothing, knowing that Raphael was too intent on his own work to notice the changes his assistant was making in the design.

And when Raphael stood back and told Andrea to remove the ladders and do likewise, he stood for a time, surprised by the work of his apprentice. 'These figures burn with the flame of vision, Andrea. Margherita saw that flame in you! That is the reason I asked for you as my assistant for this painting. In Urbino, when I saw the work you had done with Timoteo Viti, I saw a precocious talent. This goes beyond talent. Well done, my artist.'

Andrea felt a warm glow within himself. Raphael

mused aloud, 'But what you have added to the composition makes it all the more evident that there is something too empty about the lower part of the canvas.' Raphael pursed his lips. He sighed, 'But I am tired, and tomorrow is another day.'

'Please, sir,' Andrea interjected, 'may I stay in the studio and experiment with some sketches?'

Raphael touched his shoulder. 'By all means, my young friend. I see you have come to love the old man, our Holy Father.'

'Yes,' Andrea replied, 'I believe I have.'

'Well stay if you wish, and if you find a solution, paint it in outline. We can overpaint it if it does not work. Now, goodnight.'

Andrea lost no time, for an idea had already formed in his mind. Since coming to Rome his nightmares had ended, but he was troubled, in a dull, persistent way, by the image of his dead twin. Baseless as it was, the responsibility he felt for his twin's death lurked in the corner of his mind. Now he had a chance to banish his guilt. For he planned to give his brother life. Beneath the feet of the Virgin, at the base of the painting, Andrea sketched two little angels. The wind that billowed the garments of Mary and St Sixtus ruffled the angels' hair. They had serious, thoughtful faces and they looked anxiously at something beyond the painting's frame, with eyes that were wide and staring. Their lips compressed, they held in their feeling.

Andrea worked like a fury. The figures took life on the canvas. He portrayed one angel with his fingers to his lips. He was sure that he had carried this angel inside him ever since Menocchio had first spoken to him of Gabriel. This, without doubt, was Andrea's angel. And the face and expression of the angel gave life to the brother he had never known. Andrea shed tears of joy as he beheld his angel brother.

Exhausted, he fell asleep in the studio, curled up in a cloak in the corner. When he woke, Raphael was standing before the canvas, one arm across his chest, a finger across his lips, in deep study of the work. Andrea jumped to his feet and moved to his side, waiting for the verdict. Raphael made no move and then he turned and surveyed his assistant before embracing him and offering his congratulations. 'The flame of vision,' he said, and repeated the phrase as he perused the canvas.

On 14 February, the Feast of St Valentine, patron saint of lovers, Julius stated his wish to see the completed work, though he was too weak to come to the studio. Raphael feared rolling the canvas, for the final coats of varnish had not been applied and there was a danger that the paint might crack or break. But the Pope, knowing that the end was near, was not to be denied. So master and assistant reluctantly rolled the canvas and carried the Madonna to the Papal apartments.

The Pontiff was propped up in bed, his physician and confessor by his side. His body was wasted, skeletal, but light still danced in his eyes. He greeted the unrolling of the painting with a beaming smile of pleasure and approval. From under the covers, he reached out his hand and summoned Raphael to him. The painter knelt by the bedside and kissed the ring, retiring quickly at a signal from the physician.

'The boy,' Julius whispered, his voice weak and crackly, though the words were distinct and clear. Raphael urged Andrea forward. He dropped to his knees close to the

Pope. The old man smiled at him and, placing a hand on his head, blessed him. When Andrea raised his tearful eyes to Julius's face, the Pontiff touched his cheek. 'Go with God, my child.'

A week later, as a light covering of snow lay on the Roman hills, Julius died a calm and serene death and the cold wind of change blew through the corridors of the Vatican.

17

FIRESKY

Dresden, September 1944–February 1945

In the weeks following the dinner at his apartment, Franz
Heller saw Maria and Jacob many times. They met in the
gallery and then went to a coffee house or cinema.
Occasionally they attended a concert.

To Maria, Heller was attentive and gallant, and he
earned Jacob's trust, though the boy, in truth, felt little
affection for him. He did, however, welcome their outings
as a relief from the monotony of his days.

This new friendship wrought a transformation in
Heller. Now, as he readied himself to write, setting out
his pen and paper, opening his notebook and scanning
what he had already written, he looked forward to reading
the completed work to his friends. He wanted to share it,
to explain how the pieces of the jigsaw had come together.
Maria and Jacob were in his mind as he held the pen in
his hand, savoured its weight and set to work:

> Tycho Brahe assigned a small room to Kepler to
> act as his study. Barbara did not think it worthy
> of her husband's standing. After all, the Dane
> had invited him to come as an equal, in a spirit

of fraternity. Yet here he was, locked away in a room that was little more than a privy. 'Of course it is me who suffers the insult. You are too blind to notice it,' she complained.

Kepler fobbed her off with the promise that he would speak of it to Tycho. But he didn't. He liked the room. Within it he found all the quiet he could hope to get in that chaotic house. It was there that Jan and Kepler spoke.

At first, Jan was wary of his saviour. The astronomer was moody and dour. His clothes gave off an unpleasant odour. The boy did not understand why he had intervened to save him. Sitting on a small stool next to Kepler's desk, he plucked up the courage to ask.

'Why do you help me, sir?'

Kepler raised his head from the papers he had been perusing. He looked steadily at the boy, taking in his features for the first time, noting the homespun tunic and shirt, the eager eyes. At length he spoke and his voice had none of the whining quality it sometimes possessed.

'My family know what it is to be persecuted. To suffer at the hands of madness.'

A cloud of remembrance passed over Kepler's face. His voice lowered, growing in intensity. His eyes were far away.

'My mother was brought before the Inquisition on trumped-up charges of consorting with the Devil.' Kepler looked directly at Jan. 'I saw the flame set for her. By the mercy of God she escaped.'

Kepler dwelt on the memory. When he

addressed Jan, the force of his words was unmistakable.

'I will not abandon you to this confederacy of fools, charlatans and simpletons.'

Jan blushed. He had never received the confidence of an adult before. The depth of feeling frightened him. But he was in no doubt as to Kepler's good faith by him.

He stuttered, 'Thank you.'

Kepler smiled. His spirits seemed lighter.

'Do you dream?' he asked, a playful smile softening his features, as if he was embarking on a game.

'Yes,' Jan answered, truthfully.

'Indeed,' Kepler responded, taken by surprise. 'Tell me one.'

'Last night I dreamt I saw the emperor.' Jan stopped, unsure of his ground.

'Well, continue,' Kepler urged him, intrigued.

Jan drew his chair closer and confided his dream in whispered tones. 'He was in a room with strange jars and tubes. Liquids bubbled and frothed, giving off bright colours, like a rainbow. The emperor sat down. He looked tired.' Jan hesitated. He laughed nervously. 'It was a silly dream.'

'No, no. On the contrary, it is fascinating. Tell me the end of it!'

Encouraged, Jan resumed, speaking eagerly. 'When the emperor sat down, he unscrewed his hand from his wrist. And I saw then that the back of his head had metal rods attached to levers and the levers controlled the movement of the eyes.'

Jan lapsed into silence, made shy by the strangeness of the dream and the fright it gave him now to recall it.

The astronomer gasped in astonishment.

'This is deep. What you saw was, no doubt, an alchemist's laboratory. There are many of them within the castle. Have you seen them?'

The boy shook his head.

'Are you sure?' There was a sharpness in Kepler's tone.

'Yes, I am sure. I've never seen one.'

'Has your father or someone else spoken to you of them?'

Jan shook his head.

'I am at a loss. Perhaps, after all, you do have the gift of vision!' Kepler took a deep breath and stroked his chin. There were mysteries here. He looked at Jan.

'The emperor as a mechanical man is sharp. The dream of immortality become a nightmare!'

He shook his head in amazement. 'This dream is not for the emperor's ears – or for anyone else's, for that matter. No, the emperor does not want to hear of nightmares. We will give him a dream that will rival the union of King Sulphur and Queen Mercury. We will give Rudolf the future he craves! And you will escape the morose madness of this place.'

Kepler and the boy exchanged a conspiratorial smile.

'Perhaps,' Jan mused, 'everything is possible, after all.'

Heller took a break. He knew nothing of dreams or their symbols. Nor did he have any reference books that might help him. He poured himself a glass of wine and prepared a cigar for smoking. He sat in an easy chair before his collection, waiting for a solution to present itself. His mind was relaxed, receptive. He stretched out his legs and enjoyed the luxury of waiting. Quince rubbed her back against his shin. His thoughts wandered here and there. He may even have dozed. And then his mind was filled with an image. But it was not what he had anticipated.

The figure of a king, fallen in battle. A skeleton standing with a sand-glass, measuring the life left to him.

Here was a dream to strike terror into the heart of Rudolf! The sands of time nearing their end. Death's army on the march. The king dying.

Heller rose from his chair. He consulted his books. The image, he knew, came from a painting by Bruegel. One of those dark, visionary, prophetic works that unsettled the viewer. Why had it come to him? Because Rudolf admired Bruegel's work? Possibly. But there was something else, something secret and gloomy that Heller did not dwell on. He found the illustration he sought, *The Triumph of Death*.

He brought the book to his desk, readjusted the light and began a careful inspection of the painting. There was much to see and the various parts of the composition competed for his eyes to give them life, so much so that he took a magnifying glass – the one he used for examining shells and stones – from its case and viewed the work, inch by inch. Periodically, he stopped and tried to capture the essence of what he saw in words. He wrote:

The countryside is deserted. The trees and vegetation are charred and black from burning. Fires smoulder. In the distance, beyond the hills, the sky is tinged with red.

In the background, there is a gallows. Upon it swings one who tried to escape from the marauding army. Soldiers stand by, impassively. They, and all their companions, are skeletons. A man in a white shirt, clasping a crucifix, waits for the captor's sword to fall upon him.

Heller paused, unsure how best to cope with the prolixity of Bruegel's imagination. He rose from his desk, stepping back from the unsettling effect of the painting. He took a little time to steady himself before he resumed writing. With a horrified fascination, he recorded more and more of the painting's terrors.

Two lovers are rapt in the music of their love. They do not see the soldier who apes their joy and stands poised, sword in hand, to snatch it away.

A mother, clutching a child in her arms, lies dead. There is no one to drive off the dog that feeds upon her.

An unconscious man, his hands tied behind his back, is thrown into a river. A bloated corpse waits to lend him company.

A young woman tries to flee but is caught by a leering soldier.

Countless skulls are piled high in a wagon that trundles through the countryside.

The frightened, screaming faces of men and

women, naked and dressed, fleeing from their tormentors. Blindly, they seek shelter in a carriage whose doors stand ready to shut behind them and from which there is no escape.

Heller laid aside his pen. He read aloud the final sentences he had written. He closed his notebook and pushed the illustration away.

Some nights after the unnerving experience of *The Triumph of Death*, Heller recorded in his notebook the dream images he had assembled from one painting or another. Having set down the dream, Heller was free to dispatch Kepler to the emperor to see if the boy might be saved. He applied himself to the task with enthusiasm. As he wrote, he felt himself to be really present in the castle, to be walking at Kepler's side and to be the astronomer's shadow self. Without noticing it, he began to write in the present tense:

A chamberlain leads Kepler through the labyrinth of corridors. Twists and turns. Through empty rooms to a door. There follows a loud knocking. A moment's silence. Then movement on the other side of the door. Another pause. Finally a voice, small and lost.

'You may enter.'

The chamberlain opens the door and ushers him forward. The door closes behind him.

The room is in almost total darkness. A candle burns at the workbench where Rudolf practises his watchmaking. A watch, its innards scattered on the work surface, lies where the watchmaker has left it.

There is the usual clutter of objects, dimly discernible in the shadowy light, in the room. The heavy drapes on the windows. A sweet smell, like incense. In addition there is the ticking of clocks, for the walls are lined with timepieces of every shape. The variation in the timing of each clock's ticking lends a manic quality to the chamber.

The emperor sits on a high chair raised on a small dais, for he does not like to receive visitors who stand above him. Kepler notes the childlike quality of the emperor's clothes. The black tunic with the ornate gold clasps, like a little girl might choose. The familiar white ruff. And the cap, with its embroidered band, and the childish tail topped with a tassel. An emperor of gnomes, Kepler thinks. A dangerous, shrewd, unpredictable clown. Touched by genius. Touched by madness. Kepler straightens his clothes. Grimaces at their grubbiness. The food stains. The feeling of life's unfairness, that so often needles him, rises again. Now is not the time, he cautions himself.

He approaches and stands a little way off – a respectable distance. He waits.

'Well, Kepler, speak to me of this boy.'

The first wave of nerves in his stomach. Trying to find the right tone. Not succeeding.

'The boy is an alchemist in his way, sire. In his dreams the objects of day are transformed into rich symbols of the future. He is a master changer. What the boy sees, in this world, is changed into vision.'

No, no, no, he thinks to himself. All this is too rushed, too blunt.

'Then there is truth in his father's claims?'

'Yes, sire, in a manner of speaking.'

'In a manner of speaking? Do not trifle or lead me in riddles, Kepler.'

He makes a low, abject bow. 'My wish is to serve Your Majesty. May I speak to you of the boy's dreams?'

'You may, if you speak to the point and tell me what I want to know.'

'Which is, Your Majesty?'

Kepler spots the narrowing of Rudolf's eyes and the quiver of his mouth. There is danger now. He must proceed carefully.

'What the boy has dreamed about me.'

Kepler is glad that he is alone with the emperor. Had others been present, they would have sniggered, hearing the fear and dread in the emperor's voice, knowing his tone presaged a violent eruption of volcanic anger for those who crossed him.

Kepler speaks quickly now. The words are fluent, urgent. They compel Rudolf's attention. They give no opportunity for interruption.

'The boy dreams of a priest dressed in black, facing into the rising sun. The priest stands before an altar. At his feet a dog sits, waiting patiently. Above the altar an angel hovers, looking down on the scene. The space between the altar and the sun is divided by a river. The waters of the river flow with great speed and violence. A bridge fords the raging waters. On the altar side of the river there is an orchard, the trees bearing ripening fruit. In the foreground of the scene stands a great, flourishing oak tree.'

Kepler pauses. Rudolf knots his brow.

'What has this to do with me? A priest, an altar, raging waters! Kepler, you try my patience!'

Kepler does not hesitate. He must risk all. He steps forward boldly to the edge of the small dais. The emperor is slumped forward, his chin on his breast. Kepler's eyes are level with his. The astronomer holds the emperor's gaze. He commands it.

'The boy is a visionary. But he can no more read and interpret his dreams than a nightingale can explain the effect of her song. I do not possess the gift of vision, but I have the gift of understanding.'

There is no margin for error. His tone must be correct. 'The priest is you, Your Majesty. Dressed in black as you are. The boy told me the priest wore a lace collar.'

Rudolf's hand touches the white ruff at his neck. His eyes are alert, expectant. Kepler grips each side of the throne. He kneels on one knee and speaks, his lips mere inches from Rudolf's face.

'The priest is you. The altar is where you labour to find the secrets of nature. The angel above is a heavenly messenger, a harbinger of the wisdom you will receive. The dog signifies your loyalty to the task.'

'Yes, yes,' Rudolf whispers, his eyes moving to peer into the darkness beyond Kepler's shoulder. The old man's breathing is audible. The eyes return to Kepler. They are a little wild. His right hand seizes Kepler's tunic. The strength of the grip is surprising.

'Go on, go on,' he commands.

'The sun in a clear sky promises success and good health. And though the waters of life surge and seethe, there is a bridge to conduct you safely over. The ripening apples speak of hopes and endeavours that will end in sweet success. Your dearest hopes will be realised.'

Rudolf releases his grip and sits back in his throne. His face relaxes. Kepler continues.

'The oak tree speaks of your rootedness to the earth, in the Hradcany, Your Majesty, while its branches reach skywards towards the heavenly mysteries that occupy your mind.'

As Kepler concludes his words, he withdraws to a more respectful distance from Rudolf. He waits, head bowed. The innumerable clocks tick away the time.

'I will have the boy by my side day and night,' Rudolf declares.

'Oh no, Your Majesty,' Kepler gasps.

The danger-filled narrowing of the eyes. 'You will deny me the comfort of this boy.' Rising to his feet, he says, 'You seek to keep him for your purposes! You cur!'

Kepler stands his ground. The emperor hesitates, uncertain. He looks around him and reconsiders. He sits back on his chair, like a little boy, lost. Finally he looks down at his hands.

'There is something in this, something . . . I like it not, Kepler.'

Kepler sighs inwardly. The thought of the White Tower troubles his imagination. The shrill voice of Barbara upbraiding him for taking Jan's part. But there is no going back.

'The castle is a strange and confusing place for a little boy, Your Majesty. If others learn of the boy's powers, they will seek to use them for their purpose. Since his nights in the White Tower, the boy dreams only of fearful things. Things related to himself. Fear of his own future robs him of the power to dream the future of others. Allow him to return to his parents. There he will recover his gift. And none will suspect his powers. Say that his dreams are nothing. I will go to see him each week, if it is your majesty's wish, and record his dreams. Send a notary with me to ensure that they are faithfully reported to you, if you so desire, Your Majesty.'

Rudolf brushes this suggestion aside with a sweep of his hand, but he is attentive. Kepler warns him.

'Keep him here and, like a songbird in a cage, he will wither and die, his gift lost forever.'

Kepler waits for the words to take effect. The clocks tick relentlessly. Rudolf breathes heavily, turning the matter over.

'You say his gift has deserted him?'

'Yes, Your Majesty, now his dreams are pitiful, whingeing things. But he has the gift. Of that there is no doubt.'

Rudolf's tongue runs around his lips and pushes out his cheek as he considers. 'He has the gift?'

'Yes, sire.'

'Allow him leave, you say?'

'Yes, sire.'

A deep breath. The emperor searches Kepler's face. 'I like it not.'

'As you wish, Your Majesty.' Defeated, tired, the fight drains from the astronomer. He prepares to take his leave.

'You will record the visions?'

'Yes, yes, Your Majesty!' All eager now, jubilant.

'Very well, Kepler.'

And then a reminder, filled with menace. 'But mind well, Kepler, mind well!'

'Yes, Your Majesty.' Submissive and wary. And then, fearing to trust, he risks a final question.

'May I tell the boy he can return to his parents?'

Silence. The ticking of the clocks, magnified in the silence. The tension almost too much to be borne.

'Yes,' he whispers, and then repeats, with more decision, 'yes.'

Kepler bows and backs out slowly, reverently, from the emperor. He has succeeded. He has succeeded!

Heller felt little triumph on finishing the scene. The Bruegel painting niggled at the back of his mind, and Kepler's success with the emperor could not dispel the cloud it cast.

*

In the office a change was noticed in Heller, although no two people agreed on its precise nature. All saw the outward change in his countenance and bearing. Up till now Heller's body had seemed light and delicate. Now he walked with his shoulders thrown back and his eyes ready to meet the gaze of the world. And his speech had lost the mechanical quality it had formerly possessed. Yes, Franz Heller was a new man. Formidable and preoccupied. Some colleagues nearly guessed at the truth when they joked that 'Our dear Franz is in love.'

It was something like love that drove him on to complete his story and have it ready for Maria and Jacob when they came to dine with him at his apartment, for he was confident that he could banish the memory of the failed dinner party and entertain his friends in the manner that they deserved and he desired. Now, when work concluded, Heller hurried through the streets to get to his writing, to finish the story for his beloved friends:

Kepler hastened from the castle, taking the steps three at a time so that he almost stumbled into the street that led down to Mala Strana, where Tycho Brahe had established his household. He was glad to be free of the oppressive air of the Hradcany. It was always a surprise to emerge into daylight after the dark interior of Rudolf's apartments. The air was sharp and clear. A bright autumn day.

Kepler burst into the house with unaccustomed bravura. Neither the barking of Tycho's hounds nor the jibes of Jeppe could take his good humour from him. He waltzed pass Barbara, planting a kiss on her cheek. He found his stepdaughter, Regina, and asked her to bring Jan to him in his study.

Kepler was standing looking out of the small window when Jan entered the room. He turned and smiled at him.

'It is over, Jan,' is all he said.

The boy's face took some moments to register his delight and then he ran and embraced his saviour. The astronomer laughed and hugged the boy warmly.

Together they strolled through Mala Strana towards the river. Kepler felt a feeling of un-complicated happiness for the boy's freedom.

'The world is good today,' Kepler thought.

And Jan thought so too. He saw the river flowing. He observed the stallholders selling their merchandise. He heard the noise from the inns. The smell of cabbage reached him. Gangs of boys played in the streets. There were drifts of snow on the roofs. He took in everything. Felt the joy and wonder of everything. Rejoiced in the full panoply of the city.

Oh how wonderful it was to be alive and free; to have escaped from the shadow world of Hradcany, where a mad emperor walked at night like a ghost among dead things.

Heller reread what he had written. Now that he was finished, he no longer felt sure of the story's worth. He was restless and anxious. And then, catching a glimpse of himself, he laughed and felt the delicious pleasure of being alive.

*

Heller sat at his desk in the ministry building. Everything was in its place. His pens. His ink. The blotting paper. The file he had left for attention, marked 'Special Consignment, 26 September'. He settled into his chair and took the list of deportees submitted to him by the SS commandant. The special train, he read, had a consignment from France. En route it had collected a further consignment, near Dresden, before making its way across the Polish border to Auschwitz.

To Heller fell the task of compiling a list of all those who had been deported from the Dresden area. Activity had slackened in the last months. Some weeks there was nothing to record. Today, pen in hand, he glanced over the information before him. Three Jewish partisans and a woman and her son.

A woman and her son. Instinctively, intuitively, Heller knew that it was Maria and Jacob.

His mind raced. Jacob had not been at the gallery on Sunday. Today was Wednesday. The train had travelled on Monday. Perhaps it was not too late! Might his superior, the SS commandant, intervene and have him released from the camp? His heart leapt and fell back in an instant.

'What stupidity,' he said aloud. And then his mind fastened onto a new set of ideas. What if Jacob was dead?

Thus the full weight of his work fell upon Heller. He sent people to death camps. If Jacob was dead, then he must bear the responsibility, the shame, for his death.

And then there was Maria. It was almost more than he could bear to think of her. He ran his thumb and index finger across his brow. His mouth felt dry. He loosened the collar of his shirt. A feeling of nausea rose in him. He fought it and controlled it. The paperwork lay before him.

He gripped the pen and dug the nib into his precious list and, with a violent sweep of his hand, tore a gash in the paper and flung the pen from him.

Heller left the office early that day. He complained of not feeling well. He made straight for the Gallery of Old Masters. He needed time to think. He sat for a long time before Raphael's Madonna. Was it a trick of his imagination or did the cherub, whom Jacob loved, have the look of the boy about him? Heller peered at the shadowy faces in the clouds. The faces of lost, frightened children, Maria said. Of children bundled into railway trucks. Some laughing. Some terrified. Some, like Jacob, knowing what was in store. Faces of the children sent to the camps. And the billowing clouds beneath the Virgin's feet were, he knew, the coils of smoke from the chimneys of the crematoria.

When the gallery closed, he made his way home. As he walked, he resolved to give all his energy – all his heart and mind – to helping Jacob and Maria. The risk and danger involved were like a blessing. He would do whatever was required.

In his apartment, Heller peered closely at a shelf of stones as if seeing them for the first time. A wave of disgust rose in him against these worthless objects, upon which he had wasted his feelings. He rushed forward and toppled the shelf, spilling its contents onto the ground. He stamped on some of the stones, but they were indestructible. They lay where they had fallen, staring up at him.

*

For months, Heller lived in a fever of activity and busyness. He went to work each day and attended to his duties as best he could. But in these weeks, not one of his colleagues laughed or made jokes at his expense. An air of menace hung about him. A nervous energy emanated from him. He was often taciturn and when he spoke it was with such strange deliberation that few dared to engage him in conversation. His demeanour towards his superior was almost insolent. He was polite as ever, but with an air of mocking disdain that was clear to everyone. But the commandant had little time for the personality change in his best worker. The tide of the war had turned and bigger reversals than Franz Heller's loyalty were at hand. And to Heller's grim delight, he was now scheduling the return of evacuees from the east to work in factories to salvage the foundering war efforts of the Third Reich.

There were short periods when Heller experienced something like joy, especially following news that, due to his bribes and influence, Jacob had been transferred to Terezin. But then, within weeks, there came news of Maria's death in Auschwitz.

He struggled on for a short time but his will to live was gone. A night in February found him standing in the centre of his apartment, gazing at nothing. The time had come to put an end to it all. But he was afraid. The sound of air-raid sirens and the muffled thunder of exploding bombs reached him. He walked to the window and opened the dark curtains. The sky had a reddish-golden hue. Dresden was aflame.

*

Heller stepped out into the night. The street was deserted. Above his head the sky glowed with an eerie brightness. The wet cobblestones gleamed silver.

In the shafts of light from the arc lamps, Heller saw thick clouds of smoke rise into the air from the west side of town. He saw flames shoot upwards, tingeing the sky a crimson-orange. He walked in the direction of the smoke and flames. The air grew murky. Dust and fumes made it difficult to breath. Heller coughed and spluttered. He took a handkerchief from his pocket and held it against his mouth. As he reached the city centre, all was confusion. Fires burned, glass splintered, metal buckled. Around him people ran here and there. Screams, shouts and cries of anguish reached his ears. A woman pulled at his sleeve, imploring him to help her. But he turned a look of such hauntedness upon her that she fled from him.

He walked on. He wanted to walk beyond his life, beyond his past. He walked like an automaton until he was too tired to walk any further. He stepped into the entrance of a shop and leaned his back against the door. He looked upwards. From out of the sky, bombs fell. He watched one fall and waited the split second for the flame and thunder. He spoke aloud.

'They fall like snow from the sky. Or manna from heaven.'

Manna. He considered the word. Why, he wondered, had he used it on this night? It was a word he associated with his paternal grandfather, who had first told him the story of manna falling from heaven. The chosen people, wandering in the desert, searching for the promised land, were without food. So Moses spoke to God and God sent his people food. The God who had made a covenant with his people. The God who kept his word. Where was this God now? Where was the God of his grandfather, the God of his father, the God of Heller's childhood? Where was his God when Maria and Jacob were transported to the death camps?

Heller cried bitter, silent tears that scorched his cheeks. And looking upwards, he cried out, 'Forgive me, Father, forgive me.'

Calling out to God gave Heller some comfort. He opened himself to the past. To the past before the madness had taken hold in the world. To the past when he had been Franz Heine, a Ukrainian Jewish boy who loved his grandfather. A Jewish boy whose parents gave him a new identity and a chance to live. And a memory, clear and exact, surfaced from the deep part of his mind.

He was six years old and he stood with his father outside the family home watching for his grandfather to come home. Down the street they saw him approach. Suddenly he was running down the steps to the old man and his face was buried in his grandparent's greatcoat and his arms were locked tightly around his waist. Franz Heine then felt the coarse texture of the wool on his cheek as he turned his head and filled his young lungs with the old man's presence. And Grandfather tousled his head and laughed.

'My young lion,' he said. 'My young lion.'

Heller, smiling now, stepped out from the shelter of the shopfront. He made for the river. The waters of the Elbe were burning. Waves of flame ran across the surface. And now the entire city was aflame. He stood and surveyed the inferno. In the brilliant light he thought he saw Raphael's young angel and the smiling face of his grandfather. And then the sky filled with the figure of

Azrael, the angel of death. The angel's golden wings spread wide and his sword flashed and gleamed. Franz Heine felt terror in his heart as the angel fell upon him, and fire swept over the land.

It was the early morning of Valentine's Day 1945.

18

The Angel of Death

The Road to Urbino, 1513

Andrea was horrified by the ease with which Raphael accommodated himself to the new order of things in Rome. For the painter, life went on much as before and he served the Medici Pope with the same careful attention that he had given to Julius. For his part, Andrea held it to be a matter of honour to dislike the gargantuan, myopic Giovanni de Medici, whom the college of cardinals had chosen as the successor to Julius. The new Pope, who took the name Leo X, was the first Florentine to be elected to the Papacy. His triumphant procession across the city, after his crowning with the triple tiara, was, in Andrea's eyes, a vulgar display of wealth and temporal power. He thought Pope Leo looked ridiculous, his vast bulk astride an Arabian stallion, perspiring under the weight of his jewelled cope. At his side was his cousin Giulio. Andrea distrusted the haughty, cruel expression of this man.

Leo, fussy and prone to childish enthusiasm and excitement, sought Raphael's opinion on every matter relating to art. The painter was in constant demand, summoned at all hours of the day and night to the Papal apartments. True, he received many valuable commissions from the Medicis, but Andrea pitied his master, for much time was wasted going back and forth to the Vatican. Increasingly, Raphael's assistants carried out the work of the studio, while he listened with patient interest to Leo's schemes and ideas. And with Raphael bound to the Pontiff's will, Andrea found himself once more under the supervision of the detested Udine and felt hemmed in. The time spent with Raphael working on the Sistine Madonna was now no more than a dream or an enchantment.

The death of Pope Julius and the succession of Giovanni de Medici to the Papacy brought dismay and apprehension to the court in Urbino. It was a well-known secret that the Pope wanted his nephew, Lorenzo de Medici, to assume control of the city state. There was a long-standing enmity between the della Rovere and the Medici families. In addition, there was personal animosity between Giulio and Francesco, and Pope Leo, for his part, wanted to settle the score concerning the death of his friend Cardinal Giulio Chesi. The Medicis knew that Francesco was responsible for the cardinal's murder, though no charges had ever been brought against him.

Encouraged by the prompting and plotting of Giulio, Leo determined to drive the della Roveres from Urbino, by force if necessary. The commencement of the Vatican's campaign was a summons to Francesco to appear in Rome before the Holy Father.

Francesco, no stranger himself to matters of revenge, knew what was in Leo's mind. He understood that his main hope of survival lay in swearing allegiance to the Pontiff and acting in a humble and submissive manner before him. So the Duke of Urbino came to Rome, bowed and scraped to Leo and Giulio and then begged leave to return home and be given the opportunity to demonstrate his loyalty and allegiance. Amid smiles and reassurances, his wish was granted.

Andrea was not innocent in the matter of political intrigue and sensed the tension in the air but, nonetheless, he was excited by the presence in Rome of Francesco and members of his court. He was filled with nostalgia and longed to return to see his old master, Timoteo Viti, and speak of his work on the Madonna commissioned by Julius for Piacenza. So when it was time for the duke to return home, Andrea asked Raphael for permission to travel with him. Raphael laughed, believing that Andrea desired to return to Urbino to cut a dash, as an accomplished painter and a man of the world. And the master, who was both fond of his assistant and indulgent, granted the young man's request.

Andrea was overjoyed. He wanted away from Udine. He wanted away from the talk and gossip concerning the Medici Pope. He wanted to see Timoteo Viti. He looked forward to greeting Bernadetta, the cook who had befriended him in Urbino, and showing off his success. More particularly, he wanted to visit his parents. In the last year he had saved some money and sent it to them. He knew he had helped to ease their situation. Now they would see the fine young gentleman he had become. And Menocchio. How much there was to tell his old friend. During the three years of his absence, Andrea had written often to his mentor. But the letters had been governed by caution. Andrea never risked putting on paper the secrets that he knew or his thoughts and opinions on the powerful people he saw in Urbino and Rome. Now he would sit in the mill and tell Menocchio of the intrigue and jealousies he had witnessed among the great and the mighty.

Thus it came to pass that Andrea found himself mounted on a fine horse, no more than a few hours away from Urbino, on the final leg of the journey. Never had he felt happier, as he rode along, anticipating the reception he would receive from his parents. The company travelled at a sedate pace, enjoying the sunshine, but Andrea was impatient to reach his destination. However, even as his thoughts and hopes found their way to Urbino and Montecastelo, Andrea's mind was invaded by a vision, one that had visited him in his sleep – but never as vividly as it now appeared. The sky above him was filled with the figure of Azrael, the angel of death. His golden wings were spread wide and his mighty sword flashed and gleamed. And the angel hovered and seemed set to fall, in terrible fury, upon him.

So real was the vision that Andrea cried out in terror and searched the sky with fearful eyes; even as he did so, the company of the duke was attacked. Without warning, there was the sudden, thunderous sound of gunshot. And then, amid shouts and cries, horsemen bore down upon them. All was confusion. In front of Andrea, a horse staggered. The animal reared on its hind legs and toppled over, its side ripped asunder by a shot from a pistol.

Andrea could not take in what was happening. The duke's guards, mercenaries brought from France by Francesco, were quickly into action. Swords at the ready, they charged at their enemies. But who were the enemy? Local men from Urbino? Surely not. Bandits waiting for anyone to pass? No, the attack was too well organised for that. And this was no ragged band of desperadoes. Could it be that these men had been hired by the duke's enemies?

But what enemies? The Pope of Rome. The answer leapt into his mind. Leo, Raphael's patron? Andrea wanted to banish this thought. But it would not go away. Nor would the face of Giulio Medici, with the protruding eyes and sneering mouth that terrified Andrea.

And then there was no more time for thought or speculation, for the fighting was all around him. Andrea had been taught how to use a sword in Urbino but he had never drawn a weapon in anger. Now he was in the middle of a skirmish where his life depended upon drawing his sword and fighting his way to freedom. Andrea saw himself in his mind's eye. Even in the midst of battle, he realised how ridiculous the situation was. He was not a soldier. He was not wearing a breastplate or a helmet. He was a painter. A painter working in the studio of Raphael Santi of Urbino. He was not dressed for war. His linen shirt was white and fresh. His amber-velvet tunic was fashionably cut. His grey wool cloak was the finest he could afford. He wore a soft hat – at an angle, to show off his thick, wavy hair. His leather riding boots he had borrowed from a member of the Papal court. And now, an hour's ride from Urbino, he was on the verge of battle.

Andrea's horse, a dark roan mare, was side-stepping and snorting. The animal's nostrils were wide, her eyes wild and frightened. Andrea knew that the horse could sense his fear. He gripped tightly with his knees and shortened his rein, forcing the mare's head upwards. Taking the sword from its scabbard, Andrea kicked his mount forward. He wanted to ride through the field, through the battle to the open spaces beyond. He held the sword outstretched to indicate the direction he should take. Andrea was dimly aware of the screams and shouts of men and horses crying and falling. But he kept his eyes fixed on a distant hill and the patch of sky that hung above it. There he launched himself, aiming himself like an arrow shot from a bow. And in the midst of his fear Andrea felt a release, an exhilaration, as his mare shot through the confusion and the entanglement of men and horses.

Andrea did not see the man whose shortened pike, borne like a lance, pierced his side. He felt the force of the blow knock him sideways and felt a sharp pain. He tried to keep his seat, but the mare bolted and Andrea was thrown clear of her.

He fell heavily and lay face-forward for some moments on the grassy ground. Andrea rolled onto his back and propped himself on his elbow. He was a little removed from the battle. He looked upon the scene as one might look upon a painting. He noted the fall of light and the direction of the lengthening shadows. He remembered Raphael speaking of Leonardo's great fresco *The Battle of Anghiari*, which captured the twisting forms of men and horses. Here was that fresco come to life. Here were the images from his nightmares come true!

Andrea felt winded, and he had a cramp in his side. His left side. He pressed against it with his right hand to ease the pain. And then he realised, for the first time, that his life's blood was oozing from him. He opened his hand and held it, crimson and wet, before his face.

No, no, he thought, the tears coming to his eyes, no, no, no. Andrea thought of his parents in Montecastelo. Why was he here and not with them? He thought of St Barbara, patron saint of soldiers. She had been one of the figures in the altarpiece he had worked on for Piacenza. His master, Raphael, had told him that soldiers prayed to her for safe deliverance in time of war. Andrea had never liked her face, in the painting. He thought she looked disdainful. But Andrea prayed now to her with all his heart that she might stop the flow of his blood. And surely St Sixtus might intercede for him. St Sixtus of the kind face, who was really Julius. He remembered the psalm that the Pope had requested him to sing. The words came to him:

Save me, O God, for the waters are come unto my soul.
I sink in deep mire, where there is no standing;
I am come into deep water, where the floods overflow me.

His head felt light and dizzy. Sweat formed on his brow. And with an utter, blank certainty, Andrea knew he was dying. A longing possessed him, a longing to hold between his fingers a sod of earth from his father's farm. Something real and tangible to connect him to those he loved. He wondered bitterly what advice Castiglione would offer for such an occasion. Was a courtier required to die gracefully, nonchalantly? Should he try to disguise the effort of fighting to stay alive? Suddenly anger raged within him. He called out, 'Why have I wasted so much of my life in learning the pretensions of the court? Menocchio, why did you fill my mind with big ideas? Why did you send me away? Why?'

But the effort of shouting brought a sharp renewal of the pain in his side and Andrea swallowed his words. He was gasping and hot and his head spun. People, paintings, thoughts and feelings jostled in his mind. Faces. Elizabeth. Bianca.

And lying there, Andrea understood the faces he had drawn on the fringes of Raphael's *Madonna*. They were the faces of those not ready to leave the world. The faces of children, newly dead. The souls who could not bring themselves to leave the world behind and could not, on that account, enter heaven. They were the faces of a twilight world. Sad, frightened, confused faces. And Andrea knew that he would soon be among their number. The thought or, more precisely, the realisation of this terrified him. He wanted to banish it. He tried to fix on one image. He thought of his brother angel, resting on the ledge, eyes averted, meditative, anxious. And Andrea knew what event it was that the angels beheld, beyond the frame of the painting. They were looking at him, watching him die. The thought that they were looking out for him brought comfort to him, and he smiled as the life flowed out of him and he closed his eyes for the last time, he thought, in this world.

And then he was dimly aware of someone or something hovering above him, comforting him. He opened his eyes but now he was looking directly into the sun's brilliance. Something bright and luminous was before him but he could not see it clearly. And then Andrea thought the figure took on a definite shape – a familiar, comforting shape. But how could it be, for Andrea thought that the form moving around him was his angel, the brother to whom he had given life. And this thought would not leave him and stayed with him until he left it.

And then there was blankness. After a time this gave way to a sensation of falling. And centuries, it seemed, came and went. And endless seasons changed. And trees leafed and unleafed. And birds called and built their nests. And light dawned and faded. And still the angel watched and stood by and Andrea lay fallen in battle.

19

WATCHING ANGELS

Dresden, 1996

Fulfilling a lifetime's ambition, the young woman goes to the Gemaldegalerie Alte Meister to see the *Sistine Madonna*. Walking through the gallery, heading for Raphael's masterpiece, she can scarcely contain her excitement or believe that she is really there. And then she is standing before the painting. Turning to her thirteen-year-old son, the woman exclaims, 'Look, John, this is Raphael's *Sistine Madonna!* Can you believe it!'

'So?' the boy replies.

'So?' his mother echoes incredulously. 'John!' There is an appeal in her voice. 'I mean . . . This is the most famous painting in the collection. This is . . . Oh, it's wonderful! Look. Look at the angels.'

'Mum, I've seen them a thousand times. I even had them on a T-shirt when I was a little kid. What's so big about a couple of fat boys with stupid wings?'

The woman looks at the boy and her anger flashes.

'Don't be so closed and adolescent!' she snaps.

Turning away, the boy mutters, 'Mum, don't lay all this art stuff on me.'

'Well, I'm going to sit here and take my time with

these angels and with the Virgin. I've travelled far enough and I've waited long enough to be here.'

'Ah Mum, we've been here for *ages*. When can we go and eat?'

'Don't use that tone with me. I've had about enough of your silliness, your complaining and your rudeness. If you don't want to see any more paintings, fine. Go and wait outside for me. I'll be along when I'm good and ready. Got it?'

'OK, OK. There's no need to eat my head off. I just said I was hungry.'

The boy's mother ignores him. She sits for a moment with her eyes closed, trying to distance herself from the sounds around her so that she can open her eyes and *see* the painting. She sits where Jacob and Franz Heller and countless others have sat before her. Some who were evacuated east to Auschwitz; others who died in the firebombing of the city.

She looks and allows her gaze to travel lazily over the canvas. Her son hovers at her shoulder, but she is determined to keep him away. The face of the Virgin is more beautiful in reality than she could have imagined. Beautiful and infinitely sad, as if the Virgin has spent a lifetime of seeing despair and disappointment and wishes to look no more.

Then the young woman is aware of a strange sensation developing in her head. Her eyes are drawn to the angels at the bottom of the painting. Look at us, the angels seem to call. And in the face of the cherub, with his fingers pressed to his lips, the woman sees her own son, trans-figured, anxious, lost.

And her ears are filled with singing, the sweet voice of a boy soprano. The words reach across some immense distance:

Save me, O God, for the waters are come unto my soul.

The voice is soft. But it is undeniably there. She is overcome with an emotion that is neither happiness nor sadness yet contains both. Tears begin to flow. She makes no effort to wipe them away or to disguise her weeping. She surrenders herself to them, and to the painting and the voice.

'Mum? Mum? Are you OK? Mum, I'm sorry, I didn't mean to be such a berk . . . Mum?'

The young mother is conscious of her son at her side, his arm around her. She doesn't look in his direction. The boy feels awkward, embarrassed. He wants to sit close to his mother and comfort her, and take comfort from her. But his jacket is big and bulky, and his small backpack gets in the way, and his mum has bags full of purchases on her knees. He squashes closer to her and lays his head on her shoulder.

'Look, she says. 'Look at those little boys, John, those angels. Think of all they have seen. All who have sat here before them. Mothers and their sons, perhaps, like you and me. And those angels have been faithful in their watching. All these years.'

The boy hears the strangeness in his mother's voice. He looks, but the watching angels have diverted their eyes and are pretending to look the other way.

20

A River of Joy

Urbino, 1513

In the moment between sleep and waking, there is uncertainty. Andrea inhabited that moment. There was a voice speaking to him, but it was not the heavenly voice of his angel brother, who sang the Songs of David to him. No, it was the earthly voice of a woman, cheerful and comforting. A voice he knew.

'Lord above us, but an angel of mercy must have watched over you, poor love. For how else could your battered body have kept the life within itself? And when I saw them carry you in, child, little did I think it was my Andrea. As light as a feather you were in the arms of the Captain. And your shirt soaked in blood, and your tunic torn and tattered. It was the children, crying and weeping, who told me that it was your dear self. So I ordered the captain to bring you to me and I began bathing your wounds and staunching the blood even before the physician bustled in here, full of self-importance, ordering me here and there. But I've kept you here with me.'

Bernadetta stopped her tidying to look at Andrea where he lay washed and cleaned, in a sleep that was one remove from the sleep of death. It was a week now since he had been brought to the palace, more dead than alive. And in that time, Bernadetta had tended him and willed him back to life.

'Jesu, Maria! Andrea, Andrea,' she called, as she moved and held the soft hand of the youth, whose eyes blinked and struggled to open.

'Bernadetta?' The word was hardly voiced but he had opened his eyes and spoken!

'Yes, my lamb. Yes. Oh my sweet Saviour, it is a miracle! Don't try to speak. I can hardly credit my eyes! I must summon the physician.' And the cook moved from his bedside. She hesitated and looked back, as if to reassure herself that Andrea's eyes had moved and his mouth had formed her name.

Andrea lay still. His mind turned slowly, struggling to sort out impressions and arrange his thoughts. He was lying in a bed. Bernadetta the cook was here. He was not dead, though death had come and stayed close by. This much was clear.

The room was cool. The vaulted ceiling was white. Memory stirred of his first few days in Urbino. Was this the same room? He tried to turn his head but the effort required was beyond him. His mouth felt parched. His tongue was a foreign body, recalcitrant, unwieldy. He was conscious of pain. Not the sharp pain that he'd felt when the lance pierced his side, but a dull, chronic pain that affected every nerve in his body. His body! The limbs that weighed him down did not belong to him. He remembered the face of Julius when he had sung the psalm for him. The gaunt face peering out from a body that no longer connected to it. Was that how his face looked now? But thought was difficult and his eyelids fluttered and closed.

Drifting in and out of consciousness, Andrea was aware of voices. He felt the pressure of bandages being wound round his waist. Or he swallowed drinks that brought sleep and an easing of the pain.

Thoughts and insights were given to him in sudden flashes of illumination. He was in Urbino. Bernadetta was looking after him, dressing his wound, wiping his forehead. There had been an attack. Horses and men entangled, struggling against each other. He lay removed from the battle. His brother kept watch over him.

And then he was conscious of other people in the room. Gentle hands washing his body, brushing his hair. His mother's voice speaking to him. Her words called him back from the empty wastes where his soul lingered. He tasted the broth that she fed him in tiny measures. He had to return to her to tell her that he had given life to his brother and that Jacob, his twin, had tended him in his hour of need.

And so he spoke. His talk of an angel and twins and drowning made little sense to his mother or father, who kept vigil by his bedside, but they rejoiced that he had the strength to speak. And they urged him not to excite himself, and murmured 'Yes, yes', though his words were gibberish to them.

And then, little by little, Andrea opened his eyes and recognised the faces around his bed. And he called their names and spoke to them in ways that they understood. Nor were there fine clothes or refined words to come between his parents and himself. He had wanted them to see his success in the world, yet here he lay like a newborn infant, needing their love and nurturing. And they spoke quiet, healing words to him.

A month after the skirmish, Andrea was well enough

to sit in a chair and make conversation with callers and well-wishers. Bernadetta would not allow him to be moved. Those who wanted to see him made their way through the kitchen of the palace to where the youth convalesced.

Timoteo Viti came. He sat on a stool opposite Andrea, his vast bulk filling the room. His pleasure in seeing his former apprentice was undisguised.

'How is the student of Raphael?'

'Happy when I could be his student. And aware that what I left behind here was more than I gained in Rome. I want to come back and work with you, Timoteo, if you will take me.'

'Take you! It is not a question of taking you, Andrea,' he responded, gratified by Andrea's request. 'I'd welcome you back with a heart and a half. You know that. I have been lonely for you. But I will not stay in Urbino for much longer.' Viti dropped his voice and leaned forward, speaking softly. 'All is in disarray. The duke has powerful enemies – the enemies responsible for your wounds – and they will not rest until he is humiliated.' The big man paused and then continued.

'I have a mind to go to Siena and set up a workshop. I want to rid myself of the burden of patronage. True, the venture is risky, but you are welcome to join me. Together we could do good work.'

And before he had time to think, Andrea found himself saying, 'Yes, yes, when I am well we will go to Siena and establish our workshop.'

But no sooner were the words spoken than Andrea felt misgivings. Not about Timoteo, but about his friend Paolo Rossi. And more so about Bianca, Margherita Luni's companion. It was her face more than any other that invaded his dreams. It was her perfume that filled his senses. Elizabeth had been the idealisation of all beauty, a heavenly symbol, but Bianca was flesh and blood. The memory of the day they had spent in Rome finding clothes for his visit to the Vatican with Raphael was fresh in his mind. The way they had brushed against each other. The natural way they had linked each other or held hands. Between them flowed an easy, laughing sympathy.

'Perhaps,' he asked shyly, 'I could bring one or two others with me to Siena?'

The older man looked at Andrea. 'I dare say you will not go without them!'

Andrea laughed, for the future took a sudden and inviting shape in his imagination.

Some days later, Baldassare Castiglione came quietly into the room. The courtier, solicitous and affectionate, advised Andrea to strike out on his own.

'To be at court is to know too much. To serve your prince and keep possession of a clear conscience is difficult, Andrea.' The courtier sat back in his chair. Andrea saw him compose himself for what he was about to say. 'When you first came here, I envied you your innocence.'

'But it was you, sir, who made me understand that Cardinal Chesi . . . ' – Andrea considered how to phrase what he wanted to say – 'was a victim of intrigue.'

'I let you see that I was involved in plotting his death. Is that what you mean?'

'Yes.' Andrea felt uncomfortable in playing the confessor to his former master, but he was relieved that the dark, unspoken thing that lay between them was now in the open.

Castiglione spoke without affectation and with little regard for the elegance of his phrases. 'I do not know why

I did that. To warn you, to shock you. To destroy the innocence that I could not possess. The reasons of the heart are never clear or simple, Andrea. You are well away from here and from Rome.'

'And you, sir, what will you do?'

'I will serve my prince.' Castiglione announced this without hesitation. 'We are preparing to leave Urbino, to take shelter in the court at Mantua. There we will wait. The pendulum of power will swing our way again. We must be patient. But you must settle your future. When you are well, go to Montecastelo and take time to decide.' The courtier smiled at his former student and patted Andrea's arm. 'Raphael mentioned you in a letter to me. He spoke of the angels you created.'

'Ah yes, my angels!'

Castiglione rose to go. 'Please remember that I am your friend, Andrea.'

Castiglione's visit gave Andrea new heart. The courtier was, he decided, a good man, trapped and compromised in serving his master, as Raphael, in another form, was trapped and compromised in serving Leo. He saw the need for freedom. Timoteo was right. They must escape the burden of patronage. To be free was all.

Enrico, his father, had gone back to tend the farm. And Andrea proposed that he and his mother should go there too. There was some concern, and Bernadetta was doubtful, but the patient was not to be deflected from this course of action. So, three years after he had left home, he was returning. Not in triumph, as he had planned, but joyful that he was still alive.

The route to the village followed a tortuous path, and Andrea, wrapped and swaddled though he was, endured much pain and discomfort as the wagon, driven by

Bernadetta's husband, made its slow and lumbering progress. But the clear mountain air filled his lungs and bore the promise of health and vigour. And nothing could rob him of the delicious expectation that he entertained.

He saw himself sitting in the mill, conversing with Menocchio, telling him of the world beyond the mountain. He heard, in the ear of his mind, the muted sound of the waterwheel and felt the cool of the storeroom.

There were other pleasures to be considered. He looked forward to going to the fields with his father. He saw the two of them working side by side down the lines of vegetables, weeding and thinning as they went. A smile softened his features as he remembered the longing he had, as he lay wounded and dying, to hold between his fingers a sod of earth from his father's farm, the rich black earth of his home-place.

And then there was the prospect of Siena. Of working with Timoteo Viti. And Paolo. And Bianca. He voiced her name, 'Bianca'. Closing his eyes, he repeated it over and over, 'Bianca. Bianca.'

Lying in the wagon, Andrea knew that life was there for him. There was everything to live for, everything to learn. And there were angels to paint, sculpt and carve. Azrael, the angel of death, had swept low and touched him with his fiery breath, but he had passed on. And now the future stretched into the distance, like a river of joy.

21

EPILOGUE

Dublin, 1996

'Grandad, are we going to have our day out in the gallery?'

'Certainly, Benjamin. This Saturday, if you're free.'

'That would be great. And can I bring a friend?'

'By all means. Do I know him?'

'No.'

'Oh.'

'And it's not a "he"!'

'Oh, I see. Well, certainly you may bring your young lady friend.'

'And Grandad . . . '

'Yes?'

'No teasing!'

'Benjamin! Would I?'

'Yes!'

*

The morning is bright and clear. The last Saturday in April. The cherry blossoms are in full bloom.

They take a short cut through the Green. It is quiet and calm. They emerge at the memorial arch and turn right. The railings are hung with paintings. The artists stand by, like proud parents at a school concert. They stop to look at some. Jacob asks Tracey, Ben's friend, her opinion of them.

'Oh, they're lovely,' she says, training an eye on the formidable lady hovering close by.

'Indeed! My view entirely,' Jacob agrees, mischievously.

They stroll on. The morning traffic is building up. A line of horse-drawn carriages stands waiting in expectation of tourists. The horses munch from the feedbags fastened to their heads. The drivers loaf, smoking cigarettes, chatting and joking with each other.

They cross over from the Green at the junction with Dawson Street. They amble past the Shelbourne Hotel. The doorman bustles back and forth as a wealthy-looking couple get into a taxi. The three exchange a smile.

The crowd thins as they turn left into Merrion Street. It feels cool in the shade of Government Buildings. Jacob salutes the *gardaí* on duty at Leinster House. A fresh-faced recruit and his bored, middle-aged companion. And then they turn left into the gallery.

Tracey has never visited the gallery before. Ben has been a few times, but this is the first occasion that he is going of his own accord. The trip to Europe with Jacob has awakened in him a love of art. And now he has an opportunity to show off what he knows!

The attendant is cheery and chatty as Jacob hands in his overcoat and hat.

'Now, my young friends, what will we see first?'

The young pair are suddenly shy and diffident.

'Oh well, if you insist on being idiotic, I'll decide for us all,' declares Jacob, making a show of deep thought and consideration. 'First we'll have coffee and then we'll see the Caravaggio.'

And he leads them through the interconnecting rooms to the restaurant, past the painted faces, which smile benevolently upon them.

Fifty-one years after Auschwitz and Terezin, the sun shines over Jacob Philip and his grandson, Ben, on a spring morning in Dublin. The sun shines and the world is good. And the watching angels see all.